Wynter's Journey

A SCALLOP SHORES NOVEL

JENNIFER DeCUIR

author of *Drawn to Jonah* and *Five of Hearts*

F+W Media, Inc.

Published by
Crimson Romance
an imprint of F+W Media, Inc.
10151 Carver Road, Suite 200
Blue Ash, OH 45242. U.S.A.
www.crimsonromance.com

ISBN 10: 1-4405-8122-3
ISBN 13: 978-1-4405-8122-9
eISBN 10: 1-4405-8123-1
eISBN 13: 978-1-4405-8123-6

I dedicate this book to my husband, John. A beautiful journal given to me on our first Christmas together showed his support and dedication to my writing. He has always encouraged me to follow my dreams. Couldn't have done it without you—I love you!

Acknowledgments

Many thanks to my beta reader, Sarah Meyer. Always ready to pitch in whether to read, help brainstorm or point out what is/isn't working. I appreciate it all.

Thank you to everyone at Crimson Romance: the editors, the art department, and the incredibly supportive team of fellow authors who go out of their way to help each other. I am indebted to you all.

Chapter 1

She was in Hell—and it had well and truly frozen over. Already exhausted from her cross-country flight, Wynter slumped from the weight of her misery as she stared at the two-story farmhouse. White clapboard and white wraparound front porch with tall white columns acted as sentries guarding the gates of Hell. And all of it blending in quite hideously with the snow that blanketed every blessed surface of the postage-stamp sized dot on the map that was Braeden, VT.

The only color breaking up the monotonous white was the bright stain of red that served as the front door. Under other circumstances, it might have been considered cheerful, bright even. But Wynter was tired and more than a little nervous. In her current state, all she could think of was blood. She shivered, thinking to herself that she should not have come.

A cough alerted her to the cab driver, waiting to be paid. Wynter closed her eyes, her trembling fingers reaching for the small fold of bills in her coat pocket—the last of her money. By stiffing the man his tip, she could keep the last precious twenty-dollar bill. Quickly, she handed the entire amount across the front seat to the driver, unable to meet his eyes for that uncharitable thought.

Cold air sucked away what little warmth the old car's heater had generated when the driver opened his door. He whistled an off-key tune, pulling her meager possessions from the trunk before he came back into view, setting her bags beside the neatly plowed walkway. He disappeared again, slammed the trunk closed and came around to help her exit the vehicle.

"Careful, it's slipperier than it looks." The older man gripped her gloved hands, steadying her when her travel weary knees and top-heavy frame made her pinwheel first toward the snowbank on her left and then toward the one on her right.

"You sure you ought to be travelin' by yourself at this point?" He looked down at her very round belly.

"Got the all-clear from the doctor just yesterday." Wynter smiled brightly through the bald-faced lie.

The airline had tried to give her a hard time. However, they didn't have an actual rule that she couldn't fly at 36 weeks. When Wynter had pointed out that it was a one-way flight and she promised to check in with her OB (another lie, as she didn't have a doctor lined up in Vermont), they let her on her flight.

"Well, good luck then. You go on in and sit down. Tell them to fix you up something warm to drink." He tipped his hat, sparing a final glance at her protruding middle and got back into the cab.

He'd driven away before Wynter could remember to ask if he'd carry her bags up to the front door. Gritting her teeth and cursing her own brash decision-making, she slung her duffel bag over her shoulder and picked the other two up by their handles. The driveway wasn't long, but in her current condition, she was panting by the time she reached the covered porch.

Now came the hard part. Sam wasn't expecting her. More to the point, he'd been avoiding her for the last twelve years. She knew the reception she'd get wouldn't be a welcome one. But that was okay. She had her trump card—a promise Sam had made years ago. Her baby's future depended on him honoring that promise. Her means of escape having driven away, Wynter took a deep breath and knocked at the big red door.

She shuffled her feet, wishing she'd had enough money to purchase a thick pair of winter boots for her impromptu cross-country adventure. Okay, to be fair, there really hadn't been much time. One minute she held a one-way ticket to Florida, purchased by her parents, the next she had changed her destination, and hopefully, the overall direction of her life.

At one time, too long ago for her taste, Sam had been her rock, one of her closest friends and someone she could go to in a moment of crisis. Now Wynter was newly widowed, about to raise a baby on her own. She could no longer afford the apartment she had shared with her husband in California. And, at thirty years old, she was forced to consider moving back in with her parents—an option she'd desperately like to avoid. If ever there was a moment of crisis, this was it.

Why wasn't Sam answering the door? Wynter's eyes flew to the curtain-covered window beside the door, looking for movement. Did he know who was out there? Had he seen the ugly green and orange cab pull up and dump out the last person on Earth that he expected to see? Was he hiding on the other side of the door, willing her to turn around and walk the five miles or so to town?

Well, it wasn't going to happen. Wynter swallowed hard, past the lump forming in her throat. Her Sam wouldn't leave her out on his doorstep to freeze. His mom had raised him right. Even if he didn't want her there, he'd invite her in to warm up and rest. She rubbed her arms and stamped her sneakered feet. He wasn't here. She hadn't even considered that option.

A little bit wildly now, she paid closer attention to her surroundings. The next house over was barely visible through the spindly winter-bare trees on the other side of the road. Sam's covered porch offered little in the way of protection from the wind. Fear clawing at her throat, Wynter eyed the glass windows and pondered how she might break in. But any rocks were buried beneath at least a foot of snow, and the only furniture on the porch was a swing, attached to the shingled roof with thick chains.

She crumpled onto the swing, defeat sapping the rest of her strength. Making herself as small as possible, she huddled against the cold wood, tears stinging the backs of her eyelids. Her idea had been to ask Sam for a place to stay, temporarily. She knew, through his sister, that he lived alone. She'd intended to look for a job, something she could walk to until she saved up enough for a beater car. Choking on a sob, Wynter realized the futility of her hastily made plans.

She hadn't counted on Sam living in the boonies. She wasn't sure where the actual town was, or if there was even the possibility of a job. Wynter was so desperate to stay independent, to keep her domineering parents from taking over her life and the raising of her child that she'd run to the one person she could think of.

"Where are you, Sam? I need you." And the tears that had threatened from the moment the cab started to creep deeper and deeper into no-man's land finally caught up with her.

Hunching into her thick parka and pulling her knees up as best she could, Wynter tucked herself into the swing and gave in to the hopelessness that she could no longer hold at bay. Wrapping her arms protectively around the life that grew inside her, she started to cry.

• • •

He heard her long before he saw her. The biting wind carried the great, wrenching sobs over the tall snowbanks and across the road. Sam had been shoveling out the driveway for Riley, his only neighbor, so the woman's cries had to be coming from his place. Quickening his pace, his eyes narrowed, searching. Was this person hurt? How had she gotten there? He didn't think to ask himself who it might be. It didn't matter. She was upset. She needed help.

Tossing the shovel in the general direction of his mailbox, Sam hurried up the driveway, casting a glance this way and that. He spotted the woman on his porch swing, curled up against the cold. Her face was hidden; he couldn't tell her age. It was then he noticed the pile of luggage at her feet. Okay, now he'd ask: who on Earth was she? He certainly wasn't expecting any guests.

He stepped closer and leaned down. He was about to speak when a lock of hair, bold, fiery red, slipped from beneath her knit cap. His heart clutched and the comforting smile on his face slid away as she lifted her tear-soaked face, her lower lip trembling. Dear God, no. Please, anyone but her.

"Wynter," he managed to croak out.

"Sam. Oh, my God, I'm sorry you found me like this." She shook her head back and forth, cringing. "I'm sorry I just showed up like this."

"How did you find me?" He spun on his heel and lifted his face to the bracing Vermont morning.

It didn't matter. It was the twenty-first century. Anyone with a working knowledge of technology could locate just about anyone on the planet. If she really wanted to find him, she would have eventually. He just hadn't expected her to try.

"Pauline. Please don't be mad at her, Sam. Blame me. I … I need you."

He thanked God he wasn't facing her when she'd uttered that. He closed his eyes, emotions boiling to the surface. Guilt pulled at his gut. He'd left her. He hadn't expected to ever see her again. And damned if it didn't feel good to see her again. A long time ago he'd have given anything to hear those words. Now they scored fresh abrasions on an already battered heart.

"Where's Holt?" He spat out the name of his one-time best friend.

"He's dead, Sam. That's mostly why I'm here."

Well, that cleared up why she was crying her heart out. Sam straightened his spine, grief squeezing his heart in a tight fist, so that even drawing a breath was difficult. Wynter had found him. There was nothing he could do now but invite her in. He'd figure out a polite way to get rid of her later.

"Come on, it's cold out here. Let's get inside before you lose your toes to frostbite."

He turned his back quickly. If Wynter was looking for a cozy chat over coffee, catching up on ten plus years of life's milestones, she would be sorely disappointed.

Sam snatched up the suitcases and muscled his way through the front door. Dropping her bags in the corner and trusting she'd follow, he ducked into the kitchen on the left. He took down a couple of mugs.

"You still take cream and sugar in your coffee?" He dug in the silverware drawer for spoons.

"Yes, thank you." Her voice was soft, throaty, and still had the power to kick him in the gut.

"I've got some Oreos around if you're hungry. I wasn't expecting company." He paused to let that sink in. Hey, if she was going to make him uncomfortable with just her presence, then he needed some way of leveling the playing field.

"Double Stuffed?" Okay. She wasn't going to let him get under her skin so easily.

Sam finally turned around, a plastic bottle of coffee creamer in his hand. She'd removed her coat, hat, and gloves. Her hair was short now, sticking up in crazy orange tufts. Lucille Ball's ragamuffin cousin. Gray eyes, the color of the storm clouds outside, were red-rimmed and swollen.

"Holy Mary, Mother-of-God! You're pregnant." His eyes had reached her distended belly. How the hell had he missed that? He unsteadily set the creamer on the counter.

Wynter wrapped her arms around her big stomach, rubbing gently. "She's my whole world, Sam. She's all I have left."

Just when he thought he could get through this visit, another reminder of what he'd lost slapped him upside the head. Wynter had built a life with Holt. She was having his baby. Holt, however briefly, had enjoyed the life Sam had wanted with all his heart and soul. And Sam only had himself to blame.

Torn between wanting to take her in his arms and comfort her, and needing to push her back into a cab headed to where she'd come from, Sam shook his head and kept his distance. He'd get through this. They'd have a cup of coffee, he'd let her rest for a bit and then he'd drive her to the airport.

It started to snow. Big fat flakes drifted down from the sky, thick with low, nasty-looking clouds. Sam glared out at the steely sky and silently railed at Mother Nature with every foul expletive he could think of.

How could he have forgotten the storm? It was why he'd shoveled Riley out before he'd even had a cup of coffee. It was a break in the weather, and he hadn't known just how much time he had before they got dumped on again. Of all the miserable, rotten luck!

"Oh, look, it's snowing," crooned Wynter. "It's so beautiful." Her statement was punctuated with a huge grin.

At least she wasn't crying anymore. Sam plowed a hand through his hair and sighed.

"Snow's a four letter word around here. It was great, the first time or two, back in November. But it's only January and you know we've got at least two more months of this crap." He gestured toward the dining room, off the kitchen, pulling out a chair for Wynter when she paused in the doorway to look around.

"Well, if you've lived in Southern California at Christmastime, like I have, you learn to appreciate the white stuff."

Yeah, back to the chatty, catching-up thing. Sam didn't want chatty. He didn't want catching up. He wanted his privacy back. He forgot his manners.

"Listen, Wynnie." He knew the nickname irked her. "I'm not sure what dragged you all the way out here from sunny SoCal, but you can't stay here. As soon as the roads are passable, I'll take you back to the airport."

"No, you can't!" Her eyes widened and she closed the distance between them to grip his hands, her fingers ice cold. "You were my last hope, Sam." She stood up taller, closer, her belly brushing against him. After all this time, he still wanted to pull her to him, and it took all his willpower not to recoil from her touch.

"What do you want from me, Wynter? Can't you see how hard it is to see you again? Why are you doing this to me?" He couldn't look away from her charcoal eyes, welling up with tears.

"You promised me, Sam. You promised." The last word was nearly unintelligible as the tears spilled out and down her cheeks.

The desperation in her terrified stare, the desolation in her voice. Coming here had not been an easy decision for her. Suddenly it came rushing back to him, memories from a time he'd locked away. Sitting on the window bench together in Wynter's bedroom, the window he'd climbed through many times. Holding her hands much like she was holding his now. He'd promised her that if she ever needed him, no matter what, he'd be there for her. She'd come to collect on that promise.

Chapter 2

She probably would have stayed at the window long into the night if the fading daylight hadn't made it too difficult to watch the snowfall. At one point, Sam, not saying a word, had dragged a tall, wingback chair over to the big bay window. He grabbed a pillow off the couch and propped it up against the back of the chair, arched a brow and gestured for Wynter to sit down. She'd shrugged her shoulders but given in. When he'd added an old afghan she'd groaned. She wasn't an old lady. She was just pregnant. She had to admit, though, it was kind of nice to be coddled.

Not only was it getting hard to see outside, but inside as well. Regretfully, Wynter turned her back on the steady snowfall. It was comforting, she decided, the way a storm kept people inside. The more snow that fell, the cozier it felt. She turned on a table lamp and went to stand in front of the gas-powered fireplace. The flames were mesmerizing, and the warmth fortifying, but there was something about the snap and crackle of a real, wood-burning fireplace that made this modern one feel fake.

The old farmhouse was so quiet, Sam having hidden away in his office to get some work done. Or so he said. She couldn't blame him for hiding. He'd spent years avoiding the past and here she'd gone and dredged it all up again. Her being here was awkward, uncomfortable for both of them. Again, she regretted the desperation that had her rushing to search out her one-time best friend before considering what things would be like once she'd found him. She had tried to talk to him earlier. She figured he'd want to know about Holt, at the very least. But she guessed Sam just wasn't ready. She'd try again another time.

Wynter decided to give herself a little tour of Sam's home. He hadn't said there was anywhere she couldn't go, yet she felt a little like Belle, sneaking through the Beast's castle on her way to the forbidden west wing. She stifled a giggle as she snuck past the closed door at the end of the hall. The strip of light beneath revealed Sam's office, his hideout. She didn't even know what he did for a living.

Upstairs she found her bags had been left in a spare bedroom. She flipped on the overhead light and nodded her approval. Unlike the downstairs, the upstairs was carpeted, plush, and luxurious beneath her bare feet. The room wasn't overly masculine or disgustingly frilly, but struck a nice balance. Wynter would have chosen a similar shade of green for her own walls, but their apartment lease had specifically prohibited painting the walls of their tiny rental.

The bedding and curtains were a neutral white. She gasped when she discovered the deep window had a cushioned bench. Oh, to curl up in that spot and read the day away! She gave it a test sit for now, pressing her fingers to the chilly glass. She couldn't wait to see it during a gorgeous, sunny day. Sometimes she wondered if she might have been a cat in a former life.

Tiptoeing across the hall, Wynter slipped into Sam's room. This was so different from his childhood bedroom. No Star Wars spaceships hanging from the ceiling or action figures cluttering every available surface. The ugly blue comforter with a crude recreation of the solar system had been replaced with a soft brown duvet. She knew this because she couldn't help reaching out to run her fingertips over the smooth fabric.

The room was comfortable, inviting, but it was lacking … something. Wynter turned in a circle, approving of the overstuffed bookshelves, the piles of books on both matching bedside tables. Sam's closet door was firmly shut. She wondered if he still had trouble sleeping if he knew it was open. No clothes littered the floor. Well, that was new.

Then she realized what had bothered her. Most people had photos on the walls, on dressers or tables. It was what gave a room personality, heart. Sam's bedroom didn't showcase a single photograph. Nothing that captured memories of his childhood, of his family. Not even a picture of his late parents. Wynter wanted to cry for the boy she had known.

"You want to tell me why you're poking your nose in my room?"

Wynter turned to face her old friend. His tall form filled most of the doorframe. An unruly lock of chestnut hair fell down over one eye, just as it had since she'd met him, the first day of kindergarten. She noticed a jagged scar that bisected his right eyebrow. That was new … to her. His hazel eyes flickered with irritation. She looked down, guiltily.

"I'm sorry. I shouldn't have come in. I just wanted to see if I could learn a little about you from your house, your things."

"You were going through my things?" His voice growled, even deeper than before.

"No! I didn't mean it that way." She scowled in frustration, started to reach out to him and stopped herself.

"Sam. I miss my best friend. Where did you go?" They both knew she didn't mean here, in this farmhouse in backwoods Vermont.

"You didn't need me. Neither did Holt. You had each other. You didn't seem to notice I was gone until he died."

Wynter sucked in a hiss through her teeth, like she'd been hit in the stomach. She flinched, noting the look of satisfaction on Sam's face. *He's trying to push me away again. This is deliberate.* Instead of feeling anger or hurt, Wynter felt a deep sense of sadness—for Sam.

Again, she forced herself to remain still, when her whole being wanted to go to him, comfort him. She pasted on a cheerful smile and stood up straight.

"Anyway, I'm sorry I came into your room without asking first. I promise to do a better job of staying out of your hair."

She sidestepped past him through the doorway, her hand brushing against his at the last moment. Her eyes flew wide. The only way she could describe what she felt was an awareness. That one brief touch had her seeing Sam as a man. A grown up, virile man. Oh, this was not good.

Willing her racing heart to calm down, Wynter slunk back into the room that held her belongings. She shut the door and leaned back, her head banging softly against the wood.

She needed to get used to the fact that Sam had changed. Where once her old friend had been supportive, always willing to lend an ear, this new Sam was surly and reclusive. Her old Sam had been skinny, all knees, elbows, and harsh angles. Now he was … No. She refused to go there.

Wynter had not come here looking to hook up. She'd come to the man she'd once thought of as a brother. Only this Sam felt nothing like a brother to her. Oh, this was not good. Again, she was reminded of how disastrous her impulsive decision to change her plane ticket had been. Now she was trapped in Nowhere, Vermont, with raging hormones and a man who had no business looking so damned hot in plaid flannel and a thermal undershirt. No, this was not good.

* * *

The room was exactly as he remembered it. Walls painted a light lavender, the trim a snappy white. The gauzy curtains had been drawn for the night. A patchwork quilt, his mother's pride and joy, covered the bed where they slept.

A relentless blaring from the alarm clock on his father's side of the bed had drawn Sam into his parents' room, once he'd snuck back into the house that fateful morning. The sound was jarring and yet neither bundle beneath the quilt stirred.

Hand trembling, knowing a fear that came from deep in his bowels, Sam reached out to cup his mother's shoulder. She wouldn't wake up. Why wouldn't she wake up?

He sat up with a start, soaked in a cold sweat, panting and disoriented. It had been years since he'd had this dream, no, this nightmare. He sat up, lowered his head into his cupped hands and struggled to slow his racing heart. His jaw hardened and his eyes narrowed. She'd brought the nightmares back. It was Wynter's fault.

Swinging his legs out of bed, he stuffed them into a pair of sweats and headed for the doorway, intent on a glass of milk and a peanut butter sandwich. To hell with the fact that it was—he glanced back at the digital clock on the nightstand—two-thirty in the morning. Peanut butter was his comfort food.

Sam slipped quietly down the hall, resentful that he now had to be respectful of his new houseguest. The immature part of his brain, the part that had never grown up, wanted to whistle past her door, jump down the stairs, whoop and holler and wake the dead. He settled for slamming the fridge and cupboard doors. He grumbled while he slapped the peanut butter spread onto a slice of wheat bread.

He heard a slight sound and his head snapped up, his eyes focused on the doorway. Wynter stepped into the kitchen, rubbing her eyes. *Aw, crap!* Now he felt like a jerk for waking her up. He plated the sandwich and held it out to her.

"Ah, no, thanks. I'm not hungry … just desperately thirsty." Her smile was shy.

"I'm sorry I woke you up. I needed a snack." She didn't need to know about his nightmares.

"Oh, you didn't wake me. I don't get much sleep lately. I think it's the body's way of preparing itself for the sleepless months ahead." She giggled softly, rubbing her belly.

Sam took down another glass from the cupboard and filled it with milk. This she gladly accepted. She pulled out a stool and sat at the kitchen island, groaning as she took the first sip. Sam had to stifle his own groan as his body reacted, all too easily, to that sultry sound. He stuffed his sandwich into his mouth, his mind desperately searching for a safer topic to latch onto.

"You kept tabs." Wynter interrupted his racing thoughts, setting down her glass of milk and fixing Sam with a challenging stare. "You knew about Holt and me."

"I never asked. Pauline just couldn't keep it to herself." His sister, a die-hard romantic, had heard it through the grapevine and figured he'd want to know that his two best friends had found happiness together. She couldn't have been more wrong.

"It wasn't like we were sneaking around in high school." She reached down and began to twist the terry cloth belt that held her skimpy robe together.

"After what happened, and you leaving us … We just sort of took comfort in each other."

"Like you wouldn't have fallen into bed with each other eventually?" He knew he was being hurtful, but he couldn't help it. He hurt too.

"I missed you, Sam! Holt missed you too. He knew how upset I was that you just cut me—*cut us*—out of your life like that. I leaned on him. One thing led to another." She pushed her glass away and slipped off the stool, hugging her arms tightly around herself.

It was his fault. He had pushed Wynter into the arms of his best friend. He had no one else to blame. Oh, things just got better and better. Sam watched her for a moment. She was grieving and he'd been a prick to attack a relationship that had been cut down in its prime, with Holt's death.

"I'm sorry. He was your husband. He was a good man. You deserved to have forever together."

The hysterical laugh that burbled from her throat caught Sam by surprise. She wouldn't look at him. He'd pushed her past her limits. She was tired, fragile. He tossed his mostly untouched sandwich on his plate and skirted the counter.

"Wynter, I'm sorry. If I could bring him back for you I would." Sam paused, unsure how to ask the next question. "How long ago did he … Um, how long ago was it?"

Eyes studying the floor tiles, Wynter took her time answering. Her fingers still fiddled with the ties on her ratty bathrobe. She finally met his gaze, her jaw trembling slightly.

"It wasn't too long after we'd found out we were expecting. Maybe three weeks or so? It seems so long ago, and yet I still find myself turning to tell him something and remembering he's not there." She sounded so lost.

"God, Wyn."

He folded her into his arms, tucking her head under his chin and rocked side to side. *Don't cry, please don't cry.* She shook her head back and forth, pushing against his chest with her fists before crumbling against him. She whispered his name before wrapping her arms around his waist and hanging on tight.

She smelled of vanilla, warm and heady. He buried his nose in her hair and breathed deeply. His Wynter. She was back in his life. He could say he didn't know how much he had missed her until she'd shown up on his porch, but that wasn't true. Missing Wynter had been the cruelest torture Sam had ever had to endure.

Losing his parents had been bad enough. But they were gone, and they couldn't come back. Wynter was alive and she'd moved on. Growing up, he'd always thought they'd share all of life's milestones together. And now here she was, in his arms again, but carrying another man's child.

Dropping a kiss on the top of her head, Sam held her, memorizing the moment to replay later in his mind. His body was betraying him and he couldn't let her see, or feel, how she affected him. With all the willpower he possessed, he extracted himself from their embrace. Again, she wrapped her arms around herself and squeezed.

"You're cold. You should get back to bed. Get some rest." He reached out to rub some warmth back into her arm, thought better of it, and dropped his hand.

Wynter smiled gently. "Thanks for keeping me company for a bit. I hope you can get back to sleep for a few more hours." Wiggling her fingers, she turned and padded from the room.

He watched her go, the hem of her short robe swishing as she walked. He was a perv! Sam plowed his hands through his hair in frustration. Angry with his behavior, his feelings, he tugged at the locks until it hurt, cursing himself for being such a dick. Wynter was a widow. A pregnant widow. *Get your mind out of the friggin' gutter, jerk!* He chastised himself. Holt had been his friend too. He couldn't betray a friend by hitting on his wife, even if she had been a widow for the better part of six months.

He'd passed up the chance to make Wynter his own a long time ago. He couldn't blame his friend for snatching up the best thing that had ever happened to either of them. She had come to him as a friend and he needed to respect that, his feelings for Wynter be damned.

Chapter 3

"Where are you? What on Earth do you think you're doing? See? This is exactly why you need to come home. Thirty years old and you go jetting off to who-knows-where without a second thought, and this close to your due date."

Wynter held the phone away from her ear. She had no trouble hearing her mother's shrill tirade, nonetheless. She rolled her eyes, certain her mother could somehow see that through their cell phone connection.

Dropping onto the window seat in the bedroom, she tried to hold it together. She pinched the bridge of her nose, a headache starting to bloom over her right eye. In retrospect, she probably shouldn't have let all thirty-seven (yes, there were that many!) of her mother's phone calls go to voicemail yesterday. It only made having to make that one return call this much harder.

"How do you expect to raise a baby when you are this irresponsible? You can't. That's why you need to come home."

"I do want to go home, Mom. That's what I've always wanted. But you don't live in Scallop Shores anymore. You live in Florida. That's not home."

"How dare you sass me, young lady? Burt, she's sassing me again." Her mother hadn't even bothered to cover the phone as she dragged Wynter's dad into the conversation.

There was a brief pause and then he came on the line.

"Wynter Elise Allen, you give your mother the respect she deserves!"

"Grayson." She reminded her father of the married name she'd had for almost ten years.

"What? You know damned well what I meant." He mumbled a brief rant about ungrateful daughters that she wasn't sure was meant for her ears.

"Where are you? We'll come pick you up and take you home."

"What? No! You can't do that." Panic had her raising her voice unintentionally.

Visions from her childhood made Wynter's heart race, and chilled her blood. She remembered every moment she'd ever spent locked in her bedroom for daring to have an opinion of her own, or the times she'd been locked in there for something one of her brothers did. They didn't have parents; they had prison wardens. And the bitch of it was, they were basically good kids. They hadn't deserved to be treated so harshly. At least that was what the therapist (Holt had insisted she see one after they'd started college and she was safely away from her parents' influence) had explained to her. She was mortified when Sam loomed in the doorway, watching her closely as he gauged the situation.

"Young lady, we know what's best for your baby. You are coming with us so we can take care of her."

"Like hell!"

She was an adult now. Years of therapy had taught her to stand up for herself. However, it couldn't stop the scared little girl from wanting to run and hide. Her eyes focused on Sam. She was torn between wanting to shield him from this unpleasant exchange and wanting him to step in and rescue her.

Apparently she looked more terrified than in control of the situation. His features hardened and he stalked into the bedroom. He held a hand out for her cell phone. Wynter shook her head, determined not to cry. He nodded, though he looked stern, as he sat down beside her, taking her hand in support.

"You aren't ready for this, Wynnie. We know what's best for you. We're going to come get you. Just tell us where you are." There it was again. That tone. Like he was speaking to a petulant child. Like someone speaking to an inmate at an asylum, in an attempt to keep them from raging out of control.

"Daddy, I was married for eight years before I decided I was finally ready for a baby. Just because she's not going to have a father anymore, doesn't mean I am any less fit to be her mother. You and Mom need to back off."

"We're only trying to help you."

"And I don't need your kind of help." She tried to say it nicely, but he just wasn't making this very easy.

"I still think we should come get you. I can track this call, you know."

Fear zinged through her as Wynter considered this. He was bluffing. Please, God, let him be bluffing.

"Whether you find me or not makes no difference. I am not moving to Florida with you and that's non-negotiable." *But please don't find me.*

Sam squeezed her hand, ready to step in at any moment, she was sure. Again, she shook her head and frowned into the phone.

"We did not raise you to speak to us like this, young lady. Clearly Holt Grayson was a very bad influence on you."

"How dare you speak of my late husband that way? Holt was a good man. He loved me. He gave me a good life."

Sam dropped Wynter's hand and stood up to pace the room. He wouldn't look at her.

"Then he would want you to be with your family. He'd want you to be with people who care about you." Again, that wheedling tone.

"Holt would want me to make my own decisions, Daddy. And I think he'd be happy with the one I've already made. So, I wish you and Mom the best. I'll bring the baby by to visit, once we get settled and have a little money put aside."

"We'll look for you. We will find you." Her father's voice held a razor-sharp edge.

"You go ahead and try, Daddy. But know that I am not going anywhere with you, and neither is my daughter." Squeezing her eyes shut, Wynter held her fear at bay—just barely.

"Wynter, listen to me—"

She pressed the 'end call' button and tossed the phone on the cushion beside her. Sam turned to look at her, his expression one of pity.

"Don't."

"Hey, you don't need this from them right now."

"Tell me about it."

Now that it was over, she trembled so hard her teeth rattled. She held a hand up when Sam started toward her. He stayed where he was.

"So it sounds like Burt and Gloria Allen haven't changed much?"

"They mellowed a bit when they moved to Pensacola, if you can believe it. They weren't quite so in-our-faces when they actually got lives of their own." She grinned slightly. "Dad loves his golf game and Mom was busy organizing book clubs and bridge games."

"But they see an opportunity to control one of their children and they swoop in." He shook his head. "You'd think they would have learned their lesson with Grant. Is he speaking to them yet?"

"Nope. They really blew it there. Mom and Dad managed to push their oldest son away, permanently, when they tried to control his life. It's sad, really."

"I'm sorry you're going through this." He meant it, but he knew letting Wynter stay with him was basically asking for trouble. "And Holt's parents? Do they know about the baby?"

She nodded but looked away. "I was never very close with them, and Bob's health took a turn for the worse after Holt ..." Wynter broke off, her voice thick with emotion. "I couldn't impose on them."

Damn it. Sam paused, stepped closer and waited until she looked him in the eye.

"You were right to come here, given a choice between me or your parents. If it's hard on me to see you again, that's my own damned problem. I'll get over it."

"Thank you, Sam. But I didn't really think things through very well. I was just looking for a place to stay while I saved up a little money." Wynter turned miserably to the window. "But my plan to use the local bus system doesn't seem to be a viable option out here."

"Yeah, I'm kinda out in the sticks, huh?"

"Hey, when you want to hide away from the world, you do it up proper."

"We'll figure something out."

"*I'll* figure something out." She lifted a brow and Sam threw his hands up in mock defense.

"So, does this little girl have a name yet?"

"Holt wanted to name her Sara."

"Sara. That's a pretty name." Sam smiled.

Her little girl chose that moment to do some sort of gymnastic flip, ending with a sharp kick to Wynter's ribcage. *What would you name me, Mommy? It's you and me now, after all.* Or at least that was how Wynter chose to interpret her daughter's wishes.

Wynter had been settling all her life, letting others take care of her, letting them make decisions she should have taken part in. It was time to take her life back, and the life of her unborn baby girl. She smiled softly and rubbed the spot where she knew her daughter's foot rested.

"It's pretty, but I've always liked Charlotte."

"Charlotte. It's classy."

A much softer thump against her palm told Wynter that Charlotte approved of her name.

She continued to rub softly at her belly, gazing out at the magical wonderland that was Vermont after a beautiful snowstorm. She wasn't sure what she was going to do, now that her original plans weren't going to work out. But she felt like she'd been given a reprieve and she refused to worry about it today. Tomorrow was soon enough to freak out about her financial future.

• • •

"I suppose I'll have to make my own dang coffee?" Sam kicked the snow from his boots and slipped them off at the door to his neighbor's house.

"You have a coffeemaker at your house—go use it." Riley didn't make an effort to move his wheelchair out of the way as Sam headed to his kitchen.

"Love you too, pal." Sam punched Riley lightly on the shoulder as he squeezed past.

"Bite me." Riley raised a single finger in salute that, to anyone else, would have seemed offensive.

Knowing Riley's kitchen as well as his own, Sam started to get the coffee grounds out, only to realize there was a fresh pot waiting. Aw, Riley really did love him. Passing up the chance to needle his friend further, he poured himself a mug and concentrated on getting himself warm.

"Don't head out there until I can get some rock salt down on the ramp. It's a wicked mess."

"Do I look like I'm going anywhere?" Riley wheeled himself into the center of the kitchen and fixed Sam with a hard look.

Riley sure was pricklier than usual. Sam wrapped his icy fingers around the coffee mug and tried not to lose his temper with his friend. How would he feel if he was trapped in a wheelchair, dependent on the kindness of neighbors and visiting nurses for the most basic needs? It made his own problems much less significant.

"Figured you wouldn't be by until tomorrow. Physical therapist doesn't show until Wednesday." As far as apologies went, this one was pretty weak. But Sam let it go.

"Yeah, well I needed some busy work." He leaned against the kitchen counter, crossing his legs at the ankle. Because he knew Riley wouldn't offer to listen to his woes, he just started talking.

"She's here. Out of freaking nowhere, she shows up at my doorstep." He lowered his head and stared hard at the floor.

"Your sister? The tooth fairy? Who are we talking, here?"

"Wynter."

"No kidding?" Riley rubbed his hands together, leaning forward in his chair. "Finally, a little excitement around here. This should be good."

Sam set his coffee aside, sliding down against the cabinets until he was sitting on the floor. He'd known Riley just a few weeks when he had opened up to the young serviceman about Wynter. His neighbor had just moved in and had proved to be even more shut in and bricked up than him. Seeing in Riley a kindred soul, Sam had offered his friendship by sharing something he hadn't told anyone else. Even Paulie, his sister, didn't know the whole truth about why he was out here.

"Want to know the real kick in the pants?" He stretched out his legs and rapped his head against the cabinet behind him. "She's pregnant. She's having my best friend's baby."

"Where's the best friend? Is he still on the scene?"

"He died." Sam's voice wavered. It occurred to him that he hadn't even processed this part yet, in his shock over seeing Wynter again.

"Man, that's rough." Riley shifted in his wheelchair.

He hadn't asked how it had happened, wasn't sure he even wanted to know. For so many years, it had been the three of them. Then he'd cut himself out of the picture. He'd had his friendship privileges revoked. If Wynter wanted to tell him anything, it was up to her. He didn't deserve to ask.

"She came to you. Out of all the places she could have gone. That's gotta be something," Riley offered.

"I don't even know how to feel about this." Sam pushed himself off the floor and paced to the window, gripped the counter hard as he stared through the frosted glass.

"One minute I hate her for dredging everything up, reminding me of everything I lost. Then she gives me that soft, sad little smile and I see how vulnerable she is. She's in a crappy situation and she just wants a friend." He whipped around, digging his hands through his hair as he met Riley's eyes.

"Oh, and here's my 'proud moment,' the part where she walks in and she's wearing this short little robe, pregnant belly out to here," he gestured with his hand. "And I wonder what it would be like to take her right there against the counter. Who has those thoughts about their best friend?"

Once again, he slid to the floor, dropping his head to his knees as he rattled off a few choice expletives.

"She's messing you up, man." Riley's words held pity and a twinge of something else—envy, perhaps?

"I was all set to take her to the airport. Hell, I would have paid for a ticket anywhere, just to see her gone. But I made a promise to her, a long time ago." Sam stared at a frayed spot in his sock, wiggled his big toe and frowned harder when it poked itself right out. Crap.

"She didn't have the easiest life growing up. Her parents took 'strict' to a whole new level. It's like they had kids for the sole purpose of having someone to manipulate."

Thinking of all the times he'd had to sneak into Wynter's room, late at night, because she hadn't been allowed out, Sam shuddered. If she didn't cheerfully agree with absolutely everything the Allens asked of her, it was considered disrespect. She was sent to her room with no dinner, where the door was locked from the outside.

"I've got to help her."

"Your buddy would want that. If I'd left a girl behind, I'd want to know she was cared for."

"Ri, you aren't dead." Sam arched a brow up into his messy bangs.

"Close enough," Riley snorted, angling his chair so he wouldn't have to look his friend in the eye.

"You want someone to feel sorry for you, I'll send Wynter over here. I'm sure she'd love to cheer you right up." Grinning up at his friend, Sam chuckled when Riley spun his chair around so fast, it teetered on one wheel for a second.

"Don't you dare! It's enough that I have to see your ugly face, day in and day out." Riley scowled.

"Yeah, you're welcome for the whole plowing and shoveling thing, by the way." Sam shook his head, raising his eyes to the ceiling.

"You only did it so you'd have a chance to come in and blabber about your feelings. I'd have put tea and cookies out, but I really don't want to encourage these types of visits." Riley sent a pointed glare in Sam's direction.

Sam opened his mouth to protest, then shut it again. Ri had nailed it. He'd come over to sort through his feelings, use his friend as a sounding board. A very un-guylike thing to do. He felt like he should crack open a beer, rip off a good belch and scratch himself, just to make up for the last twenty minutes or so. And 'blabbering about it', as Riley had put it, hadn't helped in the least.

His thoughts were jumbled, telling him to resent Wynter for not respecting his need for privacy. He wanted to protect her because she was pregnant and vulnerable, and because it was something Holt would have asked of him. But Sam also wanted to claim her for his own.

He wanted to be like Riley, snarl and snap until she got the message and just went away. And he wanted to take a chance, to reach out and grab the one thing he'd wanted most in the world, the one person he'd never forgotten, the person he still loved. Wynter.

Chapter 4

The sheet made a satisfying snap as Wynter shook it out across the bed. It felt good to finally be doing something productive, even if it did nothing to solve her money problems. She had a load of laundry in the wash, one in the dryer and was considering organizing the linen closet next. She might as well. Sam had disappeared again, much the same as he had done the day before.

"Why is it that I keep discovering you in my bedroom?"

Wynter, who had been sprawled across the bed, trying to get the sides of the sheet lined up, was happy to be facing the mattress. She supposed this did look pretty bad. And if she embarrassed easily, this situation would have been a doozy. At least she hadn't been snooping around this time.

"If you'd quit avoiding me, I wouldn't have to look for things to keep me busy."

Floundering for a moment, her eight-month pregnant belly made standing up again a two part process. Wynter slid to her knees on the floor and then hauled herself upright, using the bed to steady herself. She wasn't embarrassed, but it didn't mean she cared to see the amusement that was probably all over Sam's face just now.

"Oh, for crying out loud, you shouldn't even be doing this." He sounded more annoyed than amused, as he appeared by her side, guiding her away from the bed.

"I'm not helpless—I'm just pregnant!" Wynter's voice was shrill, indignant.

"I meant you are a guest in this house, not my maid. If I wanted someone to change my sheets ... " He trailed off, looking around the room.

"You picked up my laundry too? God, Wynnie, you washed my underwear?" Sam's hands flew up to tug at his hair, his expression stormy.

"It's no big deal, Sam. I'll let you fold them if it bothers you that much. You worried about what I'll find in your underwear drawer?" She couldn't resist teasing him. The guy looked completely flummoxed.

"Just leave my room to me, okay? My own little sanctuary. Let me just have this one space that's private."

Wynter sucked in a breath. Sam had hit below the belt with that one, but she couldn't fault him for speaking the truth. Nodding curtly, she gave him a wide berth as she waddled as fast as her swollen feet would take her. Stupid, stupid! She hadn't been invited. She'd played the childhood promise card and forced him to take her in temporarily. And then, just as quickly, she'd worn out her welcome.

Angry tears clouded her vision as she stood in front of the linen closet. She swiped them away with a shirtsleeve and began to haul down towels and sheets. A small pile lay at her feet when she felt his hand on her shoulder. She couldn't stifle the sob that welled up, burning her throat as it escaped. Sam took her hand and led her to the stairwell, easing them both down on the top riser.

"I'm sorry. I live alone. I work alone. I am very stuck in my ways. I'm not used to having someone else around, least of all a woman."

"And a bossy woman who just marches in and does as she pleases." Wynter's lip quivered, as she was torn between laughing and crying.

"Just like she did when we were kids." Sam slung an arm around her shoulders and squeezed briefly before letting go. "I never stopped thinking about you, you know."

"Of course not." She flashed him a half smile, cursing the hormones that brought the waterworks back on in force.

"You're scared."

"I'm determined." She didn't like how close he was to laying bare her feelings.

"What can we do?" That adorably messy lock of hair over his eye was starting to distract her.

"Move to a thriving metropolis, where I can find a good job and an apartment on a busy bus line?" She knocked her shoulder into his, playfully. Then left it there because the connection grounded her.

"I work from home. That makes me more flexible than most. But I've never really been interested in the city life."

"Move back to Scallop Shores with me. You have family there. Your grandmother misses you. Your sister … "

"My sister knows where to find me and knows she and the boys are more than welcome to visit any time." The tone of his voice suggested this conversational thread was quite done.

Wynter frowned. She started to lean her head against Sam's shoulder, something she wouldn't have thought twice about doing as teenagers, but she stopped herself now. Sam had changed. *They* had changed. Things were no longer as easy and carefree as they'd once been.

"Can I borrow a newspaper? Maybe an internet connection? I'll do some research. There has to be something local."

"Borrow anything you need, Wyn. But it's not like I'm going to charge you rent or anything. Relax, enjoy your pregnancy. In a few weeks, your world is going to change forever."

She turned around sharply to face him. How had she not thought this through? She needed money to get home to Scallop Shores. She needed a job. She needed a car. And all the while she had this clock ticking away inside, counting down to the birth of her baby girl. She'd managed to dump all her problems, all her responsibilities, into Sam's lap.

"I have to get out of here." She gripped his knees, panic lending strength and probably a few bruises. Gently, he pried her hands away and held them.

"Holt wouldn't want you to go through this alone, Wyn. I know I failed you both as a friend. But I'd like to think that he'd give me this chance to make it up to you. He'd want you taken care of. If I were him, I would." Sam's voice was soft.

"I need to pay my way. This is just temporary. I want to go home, Sam." The panic had subsided, leaving a steely determination and more than a touch of stubborn pride.

"Let me talk to someone. I may have an idea for a job."

"But I still get to clean house and cook meals." She stuck out her chin, daring him to argue with her.

"Fine. But Wynter? Leave my underwear alone."

•••

Upside down. That's what she'd done to his life, flipped it completely upside down. Sam reached for the milk in the fridge, only to find that Wynter had moved things around. He used to know where everything was. Hell, it was his house, he *should* know! Now this little fiery tornado had swept in and knocked his quiet solitary life off kilter.

Pouring himself a glass, he found some satisfaction in returning the cardboard carton to its original spot on the top shelf inside the door. She'd totally called it when she had accused him of hiding. But the longer she spent under his roof, the more Sam found himself seeking her out. Though part of that, he had to admit, was just to keep tabs on what sort of mischief she was currently up to. Not that her antics angered him, really quite the opposite. Though he kept up a gruff façade so she didn't completely tear his house apart.

Oh, Wynter. He'd thought about her over the years, much as he tried not to. His grandmother thought she was doing him a favor when she filled him in on Wynter's latest letters. They'd always had a strong bond and had kept up correspondence over the years. His sister was giddy the day she informed him that his two best friends had gotten married. He'd drunk himself stupid that night.

He'd tied the events of one fateful night to Wynter. Unfairly, no question, but it served a dual purpose. If he didn't see her, he wouldn't remember the pain, the loss, the crippling weight of guilt that had sent him into seclusion in the first place. He'd also hoped the distance would dull the longing, the bittersweet dreams of first love. Sam scoffed, wiping milk from his lips with the back of his hand.

Wynter's pregnancy hormones were permeating the air, making him think about his feelings. It was disgusting. Just another way she blasted in and changed things. He didn't want to think, about that fateful night or about how things might have been. He was good, really good, at burying his feelings. And without trying, Wynter was even better at dredging them up.

He had to help her get on her feet. The sooner she was gone, the better. He drummed his fingers on the counter, wondering how best to approach his prickly neighbor about a paying job for Wynter. Riley took a while to warm up to new people in his life. Sam wasn't sure how his wheelchair-bound friend would treat Wynnie, but knowing her, she could handle anything Riley dished out.

"Sam! *Goonies* is on. Get in here."

Now that was a blast from the past. Sam and Wynter must have watched that movie a hundred times while they were growing up. He was drawn to the TV room, where the familiarity wrapped around him like a comfortable blanket. She looked up from the couch, smiling eagerly as she patted the cushion beside her. Sam sat down, stretching his long legs out and resting them on the rough-hewn pine coffee table. He lifted his arm and Wynter took up her usual position, snuggled up to his side. Like time had gone backwards.

"We need popcorn," he said, at the first commercial break.

"Oh, please, no." She sat up, wrinkling her nose. "The smell of popcorn makes me nauseous. Sorry. Pregnancy thing." She shrugged her shoulders, giving him an embarrassed smile.

Reality came crashing back to the forefront, reminding Sam of all the years he had missed. Yeah, he'd gotten reports from Gran and Paulie, but it wasn't the same as having his friend right here. He turned to her, finally ready to learn about her life with Holt, to learn about his other friend's fate.

"So you and Holt got married about ten years ago and moved to SoCal?" He turned to face her, unsure if she was up to talking about her husband, so recently buried.

Wynter's eyes widened in surprise, but she didn't look hurt or upset.

"Yeah, well, we were out there already, for school. Remember?" All three of them had gotten into UCLA and though their career paths differed, they were determined not to break up the trio.

After losing his parents, Sam had transferred, last minute, to a computer science school in upstate New York. He hadn't left a forwarding address for either Holt or Wynter. The trio was officially disbanded.

"Anyway, Holt had his heart set on being an actor. He was constantly going on auditions. And he was an extra a few times. Just another body in a large crowd scene. Never got to speak a single line, but you should have seen how proud he was." She shook her head, her smile reminiscent.

"Why not New York? You guys would have been closer to home, able to visit for the holidays."

"He had this ridiculous obsession with Hollywood. Holt insisted that is where he had to be. Oh, and he worked so hard to make connections, Sam." Her eyes left his, focusing on a point in her past that only Wynter could see.

"He got a job as a valet at Universal. He was also a waiter at restaurants near all the major studios."

"And you? Did the housewife thing, parked it on the couch to eat bonbons in front of the soaps all day?" His smile was mischievous, yet he pretended to wince when she jabbed him a good one in the arm. She stuck her tongue out at him.

"Alas, the housewife route was not for me. College loans don't pay themselves back, and Holt was not exactly raking it in. I didn't either, for that matter, but I sure loved my job."

Sam marveled at the peace that settled over her features, the glow that had nothing to do with pregnancy and everything to do with happiness, a life fulfilled.

"I happened upon it totally by accident. This little hole-in-the-wall bookstore in Sherman Oaks. This guy specialized in old books, rare manuscripts, out of prints, first editions." Wynter rubbed her belly, absently, and continued to smile off into space.

"You're still wishing Gran would give you her store when she retires, aren't you?" Sam grinned, wrapping an arm around his friend and drawing her back against his side.

"It's her store, silly. I don't want it outright; I want to run it for her. I'm gonna wear her down, you'll see."

"I've no doubt you'll do it, too."

Since her eyes were now closed and she rested comfortably against him, he gathered up the nerve to ask his next question.

"How did he die, Wyn? Did he … suffer?" Sam knew his fingers shook and he used the pretense of rubbing Wynter's arms to keep her from noticing.

She seemed less inclined to make eye contact than he did. He felt her sink against his side, her breath hot against his neck.

"No, he didn't suffer. He had a heart attack. Crazy, right? Thirty years old. But they told me he had an enlarged heart, and that he'd been living on borrowed time. We never knew."

"Was he home? Were you … " As much as he would have liked to know that his friend had been surrounded by loved ones when he passed, Sam was equally horrified at the thought of Wynter having to witness her husband dying.

"He fell asleep on the bus, on the way home from a late shift. The driver couldn't wake him. He went peacefully."

A shudder passed through her body and straight into his. Sam knew firsthand what that was like. He shook off his own bad memories, worried that he'd pushed Wynter too hard. She didn't need to dredge all this up again, especially not so soon. He leaned over and scooped her onto his lap, holding her tight. She wrapped her arms around his neck and clung to him. They held each other for a long time, neither speaking.

He'd thrown away the last twelve years. The only memories he had to hold on to were of a friend on the cusp of manhood, not the man Wynter had come to know. Bitterly, he chastised himself for thinking that seclusion was the only answer.

A single tear began to trickle down. Sam quickly brushed his cheek against the top of Wynter's soft hair.

"He understood. He never blamed you for leaving."

Sam continued to hold her, their movie long since forgotten. At one time, he would have seen a moment like this as a hopeful sign, that she finally saw him as more than just a friend. But that was a long time ago. He'd made a choice that had taken him out of the picture, permanently. Wynter had chosen Holt. And though he may not be around anymore, Sam owed it to his once best friend to treat his widow with respectful distance.

"Are Holt's parents still in Scallop Shores? You want to raise the baby there. I'm sure they want to be a part of her life. Sounds like a win/win to me." He wasn't trying to push her away again. He was just curious.

"Oh, they're still in the same little blue house on the corner. I do want Holt's daughter to be a part of their lives. I'll encourage it."

"But you said you didn't get on well with them?"

"We weren't close. I guess I tend to hold parents, anyone's parents, at arm's length. At first, Holt was really hoping his own parents could be a sort of replacement for mine. He pushed for visits. Gave us lots of one-on-one time." Looking away, Wynter's features twisted in discomfort.

"It was … awkward. I just couldn't get comfortable around them. They tried, really. It was all me." She went quiet once more, squirming closer.

He'd take care of her. He'd help raise Holt's baby, if she asked. But he'd keep his feelings for Wynter to himself. He had hidden them for the last twelve years. How hard could it be to just continue with the status quo?

"I've missed you so much, Sam," she whispered, as she slid down to rest her head on his chest. Within seconds she was snoring softly.

Chapter 5

"I don't need any help." Riley fixed Sam with a dark glare. "And I don't appreciate anyone implying that I do."

Sam clenched his teeth, throwing his hands up in the air and letting them come down hard to slap against his thighs. Wynter had been watching the play-by-play and found herself fascinated by the dynamic between the two men. For all their obvious differences, they had a remarkable amount in common. Both feigned indifference and more than a little belligerence, but she could see how much they relied on their unconventional friendship.

"We weren't suggesting that you need help with anything, Riley. Sam was just being a good friend and hoping you might have something that needs doing that you wouldn't mind paying me for." That came out wrong.

Riley arched a sharply pointed brow, a lecherous grin spreading across his face. Sam made a sound as though he were choking, his gaze suddenly intent on the floor in front of him.

"Oh, for goodness sake! Men!" Wynter huffed, hauling herself off the couch.

She tuned out the pair as she paid closer attention to Riley's house, trying to find something of benefit that she could do for him. Not waiting for permission, she headed down the wide hallway, poking her head into each room as she went.

"She does this at my house, too." She overheard Sam grumble. "Wait until she starts washing your underwear."

"Kinky."

The higher the testosterone, the lower the maturity level. Wynter rolled her eyes. She nearly skipped one room, as the door was mostly shut. Sticking her head through the small space provided, she gasped. Eureka—she'd struck gold! Putting her shoulder into it, she managed to get the door open enough to slip her girth inside.

The room was piled high with boxes, but it was what was inside the boxes that delighted Wynter. Books. Old books. She stepped up to one box, undid the top, and leaned in for a long sniff. Ah, heaven. For some people it was the scent of fresh baked cookies, for others it was baby powder, but for her it was the lovely, musty smell of really old books.

"Riley, I think I may be a little bit in love with you," she called out to the living room.

"Aw, hell," was his response.

She heard them coming down the hall, though the room was so packed with boxes that even Sam had a hard time finding a place to stand. Riley remained in the hallway, his body leaning as far out of his chair as he dared. The look on his face was suspicious.

"Hey, those are very valuable. What are you doing in there? Get out before you ruin anything." His scowl did nothing to dampen her enthusiasm.

She indulged in another heady sniff before she exited the room, giving Sam an unexpected squeeze on the way out. She beamed down at Riley and gave him a loud smacker, right on the cheek. She giggled as he sputtered in mock outrage.

"Darned right those are valuable! And it's a crime that they're sitting in those boxes like that." She threw out an arm and gestured to the doorway. "Those books deserve to be sorted, cataloged, and displayed. You've got a freaking library of history in there."

"You think I don't know that? You think it doesn't kill me that I can't get in there and open even one single box? That was my prized collection. It's what I valued most in the world."

Riley spun his chair around, nearly crunching her toes in his hurry to return to the living room. Wynter shared a guilty look with Sam before chasing after the angry marine. Well, she couldn't very well ask for a job if she pissed him off. But she hadn't been kidding. Those books were special and deserved to be showcased. Riley wasn't in any position to do it, but she was.

"I had plans, you know. I was going to finish out my tour, marry my girl and set us up in a big house, room enough for a library." He rolled over to the window and sneered out at the snow-covered trees bordering his yard.

"It's your private collection. I understand you don't want someone else touching it." She dropped a comforting hand to his shoulder, sighing when he shrugged it off.

"Someone else did touch it. She's the one that boxed them up. I suppose she thought she was doing me some friggin' favor or something." His eyes remained fixed on the outdoor scene in front of him, a tic in his cheek the only indication that he was angry, hurt.

"I mean, who wants to be saddled with a cripple for a husband? She was right to leave." He barked out a shaky laugh. "She boxed up all my damned stuff while I was stuck in the VA hospital, put it in storage."

Riley turned his chair around to face his guests. The look on his face seemed to dare them to pity him. He'd kick their asses for it.

"You know how I found out she'd left me?" He cocked his head to the side, waiting for an answer to his obviously rhetorical question. When they remained silent he nodded, the sneer returning to his face. "She mailed me the key to the storage unit. That's true love, huh?" He sniffed.

"Karma's a bitch. She'll get hers." Wynter smiled down at the man who was far too young to be this bitter.

"So how the hell much do you want for this thankless project?"

"Oh, I'm not sure … " She was suddenly uncomfortable. Clearly those books represented a painful time in Riley's not-so-distant past.

"You brought it up, now you don't plan to follow through? I thought you needed the money? Why the hell did you come over here and bother me for, then?"

"Hey, Ri, ease off, man. She's just trying to help."

"Yeah, there's that word again. Riles me up. I don't need help." He sighed, screwed up his features and added, "I don't *want* to need help."

Wynter resisted the urge, and it was a strong urge, to wrap her arms around Riley. The man was hurting. Hiding himself away from the world, like he was doing, was only making him feel worse. Instead, she slipped a hand into Sam's, drawing strength from his warm touch.

"I hope you aren't the lazy, lie-abed type, because I like to get things done first thing in the morning. I'll be here at 8 A.M. tomorrow."

She started for the doorway, dragging Sam with her, and turned at the last minute.

"Oh, and just because I'll be here at lunchtime, that does *not* mean I will cook your meals for you. You are perfectly capable of doing that yourself, and since I'm helping you out, you can fix something for me, as well."

Satisfied that she'd be getting the last word, seeing as Riley's jaw hung low, Wynter sent him a jaunty wave and let herself out.

• • •

They argued the entire way to the hospital. It had started the day before, when Sam insisted that Wynter make herself an appointment with the nearest OB/GYN. She was in the last few weeks of her pregnancy and they needed to prepare for when little Charlotte decided to make an appearance.

The issue was money, or her lack of it. To Sam, this was a non-issue. He'd pay, end of story. But his stubborn friend was making a huge deal out of nothing. God bless her, she was a sweetheart, but when she panicked about money, she forgot to keep things in perspective. She needed to ensure a safe delivery for her baby. They would worry about how to pay for it later.

"This isn't your responsibility," she repeated for the millionth time.

It was on the tip of his tongue to note that by showing up on his doorstep, she had made it his responsibility. But that would start World War Three, and with Wynter's hormones in flux, Sam wasn't sure he'd survive the attack. He gritted his teeth.

Heaven help him, she'd only been working for Riley for a day, and already she was channeling the ex-marine's surly behavior. *So glad he introduced those two!* He gripped the steering wheel a little tighter and offered Wynter a placating smile. She shook her head, dismissively, and turned her body toward the passenger side window, but not before he caught the briefest glimpse of fear. She was lashing out at him because she was terrified. Quite frankly, he didn't blame her one bit.

Braeden, VT, was so small that what passed for a hospital didn't include a maternity ward. Women were referred to the next major town, Burlington. It was an extra thirty-minute drive, under the best of conditions. Sam shuddered to think of just how much winter they had left ahead of them. He had a strong suspicion that getting Wynter to the hospital on time was going to take a miracle.

He'd intended to stay in the waiting room, wearing down the battery on his phone playing Angry Birds. But the minute her name had been called, Wynter gripped his arm and hauled him bodily from his chair. The woman was hiding some scary strength in that deceptively compact body. Sam likened it to the adrenaline that fueled a person to lift a car when a loved one was trapped beneath it. *Yes, dear. Whatever you say, dear.* Good grief!

She was handed a gown and a plastic cup, (oh God, did he really have to be here for this?) and disappeared into the attached bathroom. He squirmed in the hard plastic chair in the corner. The nurse flashed him a polite smile and opened the chart.

"It says here your wife is about thirty-six weeks along?"

"I'm sorry, no."

"She's not thirty-six weeks?" She shuffled papers around, eyebrows wrinkling in confusion.

"I meant to say that she isn't my wife." Sam looked up guiltily as Wynter stepped out of the bathroom just in time to hear his flustered confession.

"Sam is my friend." She added, "Also currently my landlord, procurer of jobs, and since I don't have enough money to even pay for this visit, my sugar daddy." Oh, she was taking Riley's bitterness to a whole new level.

"Yes, well okay, then." The nurse looked from one to the other, her cheeks growing pink. She focused her attention on the chart. "How has this pregnancy been for you? We don't have the records yet from your previous doctor. Anything out of the ordinary?"

"Nope, pretty routine. Passed the glucose test with flying colors. She's a mover and a shaker, so no worries there."

"Ah, so we know the sex?" The nurse made a notation in the chart.

"I had an ultrasound at 21 weeks. My little bundle of joy here is definitely not shy. We could tell, right away, that it was a girl."

An ultrasound? Sam was disappointed to realize he'd missed that. Then again, she was nearly at the end of her pregnancy. He'd missed most of it. He hadn't been involved in the making of the baby, so there was no reason he should be involved in watching it grow. Still …

"Will you do an ultrasound today, then?" He hoped he didn't sound too eager.

"Not today, sir. We will, however, be checking the baby's heartbeat." The nurse smiled.

"Closer to her due date will we get to see the baby?" Aw hell, in for a penny, he guessed.

Wynter giggled. "Sam, I have pictures if you'd like to see them. I didn't think you'd care." She settled herself on the exam table, eyeing him quizzically.

"I, um, yeah. Yeah, I'd like to see them." Something about being here, in this room with her, made it so much more real. Sam was invested. He knew right then that he was already forming an attachment to this baby.

"Sam, why don't you go stand beside Wynter, right by her shoulder?"

He looked at his friend for permission, moving out of his chair in the corner when she smiled, invitingly. It wasn't until she lay back and the nurse pulled her gown up, that he realized he would have gotten quite the eyeful if he'd stayed where he was. He coughed uncomfortably, feeling his ears turn a hot shade of red.

Once her lower half was decently covered, Sam returned his gaze to Wynter's firm, round belly. There was a baby in there. He had the strongest urge to reach out and stroke the taut skin. It was amazing that a whole person could fit inside such a small space. He switched his attention to her face, only to find Wynter watching him attentively, a bemused smile quirking her mouth up at the corners.

The nurse had left the room and promised that the doctor would be right along. The silence was a little awkward. Wynter gripped his hand, squeezed it.

"I'm sorry I've been so horrible to you. Hormones, nerves. Lots of nerves." She bit her lip and looked away.

"Everything is going to be just fine. I'm not going anywhere."

"Thank you, Sam. You don't know much I need to hear that right now."

"Hello, Wynter. What an unusual name. And appropriate, hmm?" The doctor breezed in and shut the door. "I'm Dr. Valerio, and I will be delivering your baby. I hope."

"You hope?" Sam and Wynter yelped in unison.

Dr. Valerio settled down on a wheeled stool. With one hand, she moved the edges of Wynter's makeshift gown away, while she used the other to squeeze a clear gel onto the skin in order to listen to the baby's heartbeat. Sam watched, equal parts disgusted and fascinated.

"I understand you live in Braeden. We may have to fight Mother Nature when the time comes. There is more snow in the forecast for the coming weeks, and you are coming up fast on your due date."

The doctor pressed the plastic wand against Wynter's belly and began to feel around for the right spot. She paused on one side, moved it over an inch or so and nodded her satisfaction when the machine picked up a steady *whump whump whump*. Sam leaned in closer, his lungs momentarily frozen in wonder.

"I don't want you two to wait, you hear me? As soon as those contractions start, give me a call and get me a rough estimate of when you think you'll be in. I may not be here as quickly as you, but I'll be here. Err on the side of caution." She looked sternly at them before returning her attention to the heart monitor.

"She sounds healthy and happy to me. I'd give this little girl another three weeks, four tops. She'll make her appearance before you know it. I'll see you back here next week, folks. It was good meeting you." The doctor cleaned off the wand and wiped the gel from Wynter's belly while she spoke. And just as quickly as she'd blown into the room, she was gone.

"That was … Wow." Sam just didn't have the words to describe what he'd just experienced, what he was now feeling.

"Can you turn around for a sec? This gown thing doesn't have a back to it." Wynter met his eyes, her own showing her embarrassment.

He faced the corner, listening to the crinkle of paper as she slipped off the exam table. When he heard the door to the bathroom close, he swiveled around and stared at the spot where she'd lain. He'd just heard the baby's heartbeat. He felt honored to have been invited to stay, and yet the tiniest bit insignificant, compared to Wynter, who was growing a life inside her.

Grinning, he found it ironic that the closer it came to the birth of her baby, the more nervous and upset Wynter grew. And he was the opposite. The closer it got, the more excited he became. As odd a pair as they were, they were a team. He'd help her through this. And he'd do it without letting his heart get involved.

The bathroom door reopened and she stepped out, orange hair sticking out at all angles, big belly leading the way. She looked beautiful, glowing.

She took a deep breath, flashed him a grateful grin and grabbed her purse. Sam stepped around the table and followed her from the room. Oh, he was a goner, all right!

Chapter 6

There was no way she'd finish cataloging Riley's books before the baby came. Wynter sat on the floor, surrounded by boxes, some stacked five or six high. Before he'd left (yeah, Sam had insisted on walking her across the street), he had pulled down enough boxes to get her through the day. Riley made her swear she wouldn't lift any on her own. He claimed he didn't want a lawsuit on his hands if something were to happen to the baby.

She ran her fingertips lightly over a book with original Matthew Brady photos. She never really cared for military history, but found herself paging through Riley's old collection while she worked. Reading first-hand accounts really brought the horrors to life. Especially these tomes on the Civil War. Brother fighting brother. She swallowed past the lump in her throat. Hormones.

The baby sent a sharp judo kick to her ribs, leading Wynter to wonder if it was too early to put the kid on time out. Rubbing her sore side, she reached for her bottle of water and tried to stretch all the kinks out of her back. As she was still sitting on the floor, this was trickier than it seemed.

Abandoning the boxes of books for a moment, Wynter chose a sturdier-looking stack to lean against, taking a brief water break. Riley would have something snarky to say, if he happened to pass the doorway and see her reclining amid the boxes. But fortunately, Riley was avoiding her. Probably for fear of her chatting him up. And he'd be right. She giggled. It was fun to torment the slightly younger man.

The baby kicked again and she began to rub soft circles against her belly, something that she'd found soothed her little ninja. She hummed a lullaby, trying not to panic as she realized just how quickly she'd be crooning to the little one wrapped in her arms instead of her belly. Holt would have said something like, *It's almost show time!*

Wynter leaned her head back and closed her eyes, frowning. She'd felt like a fraud, talking about Holt the other night. Sam didn't ask about their marriage. Why would he? Yet she still felt like she'd deliberately misled him when she let him comfort her over the loss of her husband. Her frown deepened and her back teeth clenched.

Yes, she'd loved Holt. But not the way he deserved. Not the way a wife should love her husband. She opened her eyes, peering guiltily toward the open door to the hallway. The coast was still clear.

The truth of the matter was, Wynter had felt lost, adrift, after Sam disappeared. He wasn't just a part of her life, he was a part of her. She'd been denied a chance to talk him into staying. It had been his choice to leave her, and that made the hurt so much worse.

Holt had been hurting, too. Sam was his best friend. He'd wanted the chance to help him through this difficult time of mourning his parents. But their friend had shut them both out, pushed them away and ran. So they turned to each other for comfort.

Wynter supposed Holt's feelings for her had developed over time. They were inseparable, after all. Only she had never felt that magical connection. It was crazy, because she'd never had romantic feelings for Sam, but something told her that, given time, she could give Sam her heart, her whole heart.

Instead, she'd gone with the flow, let things with Holt develop, always feeling like part of her was missing. When he asked her to marry him, she saw it as the next logical step, somehow never seeing herself falling absolutely head over heels for anyone. Might as well give her future to someone she could trust to care for her.

So why, now that she'd found Sam, did she feel as though her whole life since he'd left was a sham? She gulped from her bottle of water, willing the fluid to wash away the dirty residue of guilt that clung to her. Tears pricked at her eyelids, sharp and stinging. She took a calming breath, then another, pushing the air from her nostrils until she felt empty.

It was Sam's reaction to the baby, the way he'd acted so excited in the doctor's office the other day. She'd found herself charmed at his enthusiasm, the wonder on his face. He was so protective of her, of the baby. He was eager for little Charlotte's arrival.

Oh, it wasn't as if Holt hadn't been over the moon when he learned they were expecting. He'd been the proudest papa Wynter had ever seen. That very first night, he'd stayed up late making up a long list of baby names. He'd bought a stack of books on pregnancy and parenting, wanting to learn all he could.

Struggling with morning sickness, Wynter had been a horrible grouch. She remembered blaming it all on Holt. He'd pushed her for a baby. He was the reason her boobs hurt so bad, the reason she started every day with a mad dash to the toilet bowl. Never actually voicing it out loud, she kept the bitter resentment to herself.

Through it all, Holt had been the most supportive husband any woman could have asked for. Always ready with a package of saltines and a cup of weak tea, his attentive concern would make her feel even worse for her mean thoughts. He went out of his way to make her life easier.

Which made it all the harder when it came time for the first ultrasound, the first time Wynter would see the baby, barely a week since Holt had died. He should have been there. He would have delighted in seeing the slight movement, hearing the heartbeat.

This baby may have been conceived to appease a man who would never have 100% of her heart, but from the moment she saw her daughter on screen, Wynter knew she would love her enough for two parents, with a fierce devotion that only a mother could understand.

And then there was Sam. The longer she spent with him, the harder it was to deny that he still held a piece of her that had never belonged to Holt. When she and Sam had listened to the baby's heartbeat, Wynter's own heart had beat faster. It swelled as she watched Sam's eyes grow wide in amazement. It had squeezed and twisted at his disappointment when he learned they wouldn't be watching an ultrasound that day.

This man, who was not her baby's father, was getting far more of her than her own husband had. Fat tears finally slipped through her defenses to roll down her cheeks. Damn, damn hormones! She thought she'd been quiet, but her crying had alerted Riley, who sat in the doorway, glaring at her.

"Aw, hell! You did it, didn't you? You went and moved a box and now you're hurt." He turned his chair and started down the hallway.

"No! I'm fine. Wait a minute, Riley. Damn it, I can't move as fast as you." She grappled for the edge of a box, to lift herself from the floor.

Riley was mumbling about whether to call Sam or the ambulance. She had to get to him before he reached the phone. Good grief. *I'm getting my workout today*, she thought, as she hurried to intercept the marine-on-wheels.

•••

He had just reached his driveway after walking Wynter across to Riley's house, before the delivery truck pulled in. Sam nodded to the driver and stood back as the man opened the double back doors. Lots of boxes. Sure didn't look like what he'd ordered online. Which meant he had a lot of assembling to do.

Thank God he'd asked Riley to invite his new employee to stay for dinner. Sure, he probably owed the guy a kidney now, but at least he'd bought himself some time. This was an all or nothing project. He needed to be done before Wynter got home. *Home. Yeah, he liked how that sounded.*

The delivery men carried the bulky boxes up to the spare room across from Wynter's, accepted their tip and were gone in a matter of minutes. Sam rubbed his hands together, his grin stretching just a little wider. No time to paint the room, so the neutral beige would just have to do. But little Charlotte Grayson was about to get the sweetest nursery her honorary Uncle Sam (*okay, he might need to rethink that title*) could give her.

Chewing on his lower lip, he scanned the room, trying to judge the best use of space. The crib would take up the most room and was in the largest box, so he tackled that first. A half hour or so into it, Sam decided it was too quiet. He was used to working with music on in the background. Something twangy but upbeat. Propping the crib rails up against the wall, he ran down to his office for his iPod.

Much better. He bopped his head to the beat, as a country singer crooned about getting lost down a backcountry road. Glancing up at the window, he saw fat snowflakes coming down. When they were this big, they usually petered out before too long. But it was enough to ratchet up his tension level. Worry snaked through his veins, had him scratching at his arms, his scalp, wanting to wriggle out of his own skin. The closer it got to Wynter's due date, the more convinced he became that they were not going to make it to the hospital in time.

Sam was scared for his friend, scared for the innocent life she carried. He stuck out his chin and glared out the window. If he had to, he'd deliver the baby himself. His stomach a little queasy, he made a mental note to Google home births. He wasn't going to let any harm come to either of them. Not on his watch.

He gave the screwdriver another hard twist and set it aside, testing the rail on the crib. Down. Up. Not bad for a freelance software game developer. One piece of furniture down, three more to go. Sam tossed the cardboard box into the hallway and tackled the changing table next.

His growling stomach sent him downstairs right at noon. He was in a groove, so he barely took the time to slap a little peanut butter on a couple of slices of wheat bread. Foregoing a plate, Sam snagged a banana off the counter and headed for the stairs. He looked briefly from the banana to the sandwich, wondering if he had enough time or interest to slice up the banana and toss it inside the bread. No on both counts. Shrugging his shoulders, Sam had nearly finished the sandwich before he reached the new nursery.

Leaning against the doorframe, he smiled. It was coming together. He hoped to heck that Wynter's tastes hadn't changed over the years. He'd gone with a cherry wood set. The light walls really offset the dark wood tones in the furniture. Glossy. Classy. Satisfied, he stepped into the room, looking from the crib to the now-completed changing table.

No. They were both too close to the window. There could be a draft. Charlotte might get sick. He rolled the crib two feet closer to the door and placed the changing table on the adjoining wall. Yeah. That worked. The dresser could go under the giant window. The dresser that was going to be a pain in the rear to put together. One of the reasons he'd broken for lunch was seeing the gazillion pieces that went with it. Somehow Sam didn't think most people chose to put their entire nursery together in one day. He was nuts.

The box of dresser bits and pieces lay open, a more complicated jigsaw puzzle Sam had never seen. He abandoned it in favor of the glider and ottoman. Surely those would be easier. Then again, maybe not.

His back ached, his butt was asleep, and his knees made awful cracking noises when he finally stood up to turn on the overhead light. He arched his spine, which crackled and popped. He was a walking breakfast cereal! His original idea had been to offer the large soaking tub in his master bath up to Wynter, who would likely be just as uncomfortable as he was by day end. But now he just might have to fight her for it.

Aw, crap. As though he were thrust into a darkened movie theater, images of Wynter, in his bathtub, assaulted him. Her flaming red hair and pale, creamy shoulders just visible above a sea of bubbles. And because his imagination liked to torment him, it threw in a few more teasing details, like flickering candlelight and the calming scent of lavender.

He could almost feel the heat from the water. If he slipped in behind her, there'd be room for them both. He'd draw her up against his chest, watching the steam from the bath curl the little hairs at the nape of her neck. He'd reach around to pull her even closer … and her very round, very pregnant belly would slap him back into reality. What the hell had he been thinking? Wynter was off-limits. Pregnant Wynter? Even more so.

Sam staggered back to the last box on the floor. He figured he had another couple of hours before he had to run over to Riley's. Just as he'd predicted, the snow hadn't lasted more than an hour. But that didn't mean it wasn't slippery out there. Wynter would need extra help navigating the dark driveways.

It took him just under two hours, but he finished putting the little dresser together. He tied the cushions onto the rocking chair and dug through the bags for the frou-frou things that went on the crib. A white crib sheet and red toile-print comforter. Wynter hated pink. He hoped she'd be pleased that he remembered that. And the finishing touch? A mobile with whimsical little owls. Back in school, Wynter had collected owls.

Well, it was too late to change anything now. She'd love it or she'd hate it. Sam collected the boxes, bags, and the rest of the garbage, tossing it in the basement for the time being. He debated whether he should take her up here or just wait and let her discover it on her own. She did love to snoop—okay, *explore*. And if Sam knew his friend, her stubborn pride would need time to absorb the gesture, without him hovering for approval. Throwing on his navy blue parka, he tried to get his nerves under control before he got to Riley's back door.

Chapter 7

Too much snow. The town was too far away. The town wasn't even big enough to call a town. Wynter sank further beneath the bubbles as she mentally listed all the reasons she couldn't stay here in Vermont. Absolutely none of her reasons had anything to do with Sam. Sam was … God, she didn't even deserve a friend as amazing as Sam. She laid her head back against the bathtub tile and blew her damp bangs out of her eyes.

The guy was supposed to be on deadline, he'd told her often enough over the past few days. And yet he'd taken the time, the whole day, she supposed, to create a cozy paradise for her incredibly lucky little girl. She should have been angry at the expense. It was her responsibility, after all. Goodness knew they'd been arguing about that since the day she'd barged back into his life. But the gesture, the sweetest, kindest gesture, was not something she could throw back in his face.

Twelve years they'd been apart. Twelve years and yet he remembered her so well. Sam knew she'd gag over any Pepto-Bismol-girlie-pink in her daughter's nursery. The toile was country chic, not teddy-bear-cutesy, and paired well with the dark wood furniture. She would find a way, later, to explain that they would have to leave the comforter out of the crib once Charlotte was actually using it. For now, it stayed, as a reminder of Sam's incredible generosity and loving heart. Wynter had even spent a few quiet moments rocking away in her new glider, admiring his hard work.

The warm water relaxed her tired, aching muscles. Her body began to unwind. But her brain was on overtime. It was getting harder to hang on to the desperate determination to get back to Scallop Shores. The temptation to stay and play house with

Sam crowded her thoughts. She closed her eyes and breathed in the lavender soap that she'd used as a substitute for bubble bath. Surprisingly enough, it created nearly as many bubbles as the real stuff.

Oh, Sam. He'd started out a means to an end. He'd left them, after all. She'd intended to harden her heart against her former best friend, lest it break again when it was time to leave. But he'd had to go and make her feel welcome. He'd had to go and get attached to her unborn baby. Oh, he could try to deny it, but Wynter knew the truth. Her Sam might have left Scallop Shores behind to hide out in the middle of nowhere, but he hadn't changed so much. He was still the most amazing guy she knew.

Lifting a foot from the water, she finally caught sight of something she hadn't seen for a while: her toes. Wynter grinned. She rubbed her belly in long, slow strokes. Concentrating on the warmth of the water, the moist air, and the strong scent of lavender, it was almost possible to fully relax. Her first-time parent fears, the thought of being a single mom with no real job to speak of, receded to the back of her brain. Her worries were more of a faint buzz, at the moment, than the cymbal-smashing marching band that tromped through her head most of the day.

"Everything okay in there?" Sam's baritone rumbled through the door.

She knew he wouldn't open the door unless he was 100 percent certain that she was in danger, yet Wynter found herself rearranging bubbles to protect her modesty.

"We're just fine. Thank you for letting me use this soaking tub, Sam. I'm not sure I ever want to get out."

"Uh huh. Tell me that after the water's cooled off." His footsteps receded, faintly scuffing across the carpet.

Wynter stroked her stomach again. "Oh, little girl, I want to be a mommy you can be proud of. I want to be the kind of mommy your daddy thought I'd be." She smiled at the answering thump.

Wynter soaked a washcloth in the hot water, wrung it out and placed it over her eyes. That felt good. She closed her eyes and conjured her 'happy place,' the future she envisioned for her and Charlotte. They would each have their own room in the small apartment above Sam's grandmother's bookstore in Scallop Shores. Charlotte would come to work with her. What a place to grow up in!

She'd spent much of her own teen years hanging out in The Book Nook. As soon as she was old enough, Sam's grandmother hired her to man the cash register, giving the other employees a chance to take their lunch breaks or stock the shelves. She wasn't actually given very many hours, but that didn't stop her from spending most of her free time there. When surrounded by books, especially in the used section, Wynter was at her happiest.

Ah, the thought of finally settling in Scallop Shores, getting reacquainted with the locals, being welcomed back into the fold and feeling as though she'd never really left. In her head Wynter walked the streets, so quiet in the winter but getting more crowded as tourists started to filter in for the summer months. She remembered the Civil War statue in the center of town, the beautiful cemeteries, and the old churches. In the summer there were flowers everywhere; in the winter the snow and ice decorated the bare tree limbs. Oh, she couldn't wait to go back.

When she'd first come up with the idea of asking Sam for a place to stay until she could save up enough to move back home, including him in her plans for the future never even crossed her mind. Foolishly, she found herself trying to reserve him a spot, a spot he didn't want. Sam would never come with her. At least she knew where he lived now. She could always visit. But it wouldn't be the same.

The washcloth over her eyes had grown cool. Her happy place was no longer quite as happy. Uncovering her eyes, she found that most of the bubbles had dissipated. Sam would be waiting for his turn to use the tub, or at the very least, for her to leave his bathroom, as she'd have to cross through his bedroom to do so.

Unbidden, the thought of Sam lying in his bed as she exited the bathroom came to mind. Though the bath water had begun to cool, Wynter's skin felt flushed and tingly. What did he wear to bed? He didn't seem like a pajama kind of guy. Boxers or briefs, Sam?

She wanted to giggle, but her throat was clogged. Need? Frustration? Bracing herself against the sides of the tub, she used the buoyancy of the water to push herself to a standing position. The last thing she needed was to have to holler out to Sam to come rescue her from the bathtub.

Wynter reached for the snowy white towel. Drying off suddenly felt torturous as her skin was entirely too sensitive. Frustrated, she stuffed a corner of the towel between her teeth and bit down, resisting the urge to scream. She glared at the closed door leading to Sam's bedroom.

Why Sam? And why now? Her pregnancy hormones were supposed to make her cry, not want to throw her elephantine self at her best friend. It was crazy. She was crazy. She sniffled. It came out as half-sob, half-laugh but the tears did come. She didn't think to mask the sound.

This time his fist pounded on the door. "What's wrong? Are you hurt? Cover up—I'm coming in!"

She had just enough time to throw the towel around her middle, tucking it between her breasts, before Sam came barreling in. A hand covered his eyes, though he peeked between two fingers. The tears continued to course down her cheeks, though she'd be darned if she knew exactly why. Sam's hands skimmed her arms, held her away as he looked her over for some perceived damage.

If she'd thought she knew torture before, toweling off was nothing compared to being this close to him, having his hands on her. This time she howled her frustration, taking cover behind the tears. Sam wrapped her in his arms, murmuring soothing words as he guided her out of the bathroom and into his room. He paused, perhaps contemplating whether he should deposit her in his own bed, as it was closer. God, no!

Wynter kept her feet moving, dragging Sam along with her. His long arm around her shoulders, they made quite a pair, shuffling down the hall. His voice was low and soft in her ear. She wasn't even sure what he was saying. He probably couldn't have said either. But it wasn't helping, the deep timbre and the rolling rhythm. She gripped the edges of the terrycloth towel together and willed herself not to lose control.

Sam led her into the bedroom, moving purposely to the bed and yanking down the covers. It wasn't until he'd turned around that he must have remembered that she was still basically soaking wet. Shivering, she waited in the center of the room.

"Um, do you need any help getting dried off?" The Adam's apple in Sam's throat bobbed as he focused his attention on a point just over Wynter's left shoulder.

"I'm good. Thanks." She sniffled.

"Okay then. I'll give you a few minutes to get into a nightgown, then I'm coming back to check on you." His voice held a gravelly edge.

As soon as the door shut, Wynter whisked the towel off, rubbing herself dry, before putting on a thick flannel nightgown. There. Hard to think sexy thoughts when you looked like Little Red Riding Hood's grannie. Well, hard but not impossible. She slipped into bed, pulling the covers up to her chin and tried to calm her racing hormones. She wasn't sure quite how much time had passed when Sam knocked softly at the door. She snapped her eyelids shut, feigning sleep.

She listened to his footsteps cross the threshold, stopping beside the bed. The mattress dipped as he sat down, the back of his hand coming to rest against her forehead. Concentrating on breathing slowly, in and out, in and out, Wynter squelched the shiver that would give her away. She could feel the warmth from his body as he leaned down.

And then he kissed her. His lips were soft against hers, full of promise and hope. She felt like Snow White and Cinderella, every fairy tale princess there ever was. She wanted to open her eyes and invite him into her heart, into her bed. But she hadn't even given this much of herself to Holt, her husband. She'd held back with him. He'd deserved so much more than she'd given him. Reminded of the half-life she'd had with Holt, Wynter continued to breathe deep. *Go away, Sam. I don't deserve you, Sam.*

"Sweet dreams, Wyn." He brushed a knuckle against her cheek before leaving.

• • •

He'd log way more productive hours if he just put a coffee maker in his office. Sam headed back down the hall from the kitchen, his third cup of coffee quickly cooling off. But then he'd need a mini fridge for his milk. It wasn't worth the hassle.

Setting the mug down on his desk, he slumped into his chair and scowled at the computer screen. His five o'clock deadline was in four hours and he had to figure out how to squeeze about ten hours of work into that time frame. He could do it, no question. But it disgusted him that he'd let things get down to the wire like this.

It was too quiet. Wynter was at Riley's, cataloging old mildewy books. He was stuck here with hours of endless coding. Not that he wanted to be at his neighbor's. Nor did he want to be around mildewy books. He just wanted to be around her. Damn it. He'd spent twelve years hiding from her and in just a few weeks he was her little lap hound. Pathetic.

And it wasn't like it was reciprocated. He'd tested out that theory last night. God, she'd scared the hell out of him when he heard her sobbing in his bathroom. Seeing her in only a towel, the front of which would not pull entirely together, Sam had almost swallowed his tongue.

He still wasn't sure what Wynter had been crying about, but she wasn't bleeding, she wasn't hobbling, and she wasn't worried about the baby. His head told him to tuck her into bed and make sure she got some rest. His body told him different, as he breathed in the scent of lavender radiating from her dewy skin. Her sun-kissed hair stuck out at all angles and her skin was glowing a gorgeous pink.

Be a gentleman. Be a gentleman. She's about ready to give birth, for crying out loud! He'd gotten her to her room. She was safe and sound. He should have left it at that. But he'd gone back in. No way could she have fallen asleep that fast. She was faking. And the fact that she hadn't reacted when he kissed her? She was being kind.

Sam knocked his coffee mug on a tooth when he brought it up to his mouth too fast. The liquid was now tepid. Add a damned microwave to the list of things he needed in order to run an efficient business and not have to keep leaving this room. He set the cup down, pushing it to the edge of the desk. He didn't need it. He was just looking for excuses to get up and think about his temporary housemate.

There. Temporary. *Just keep that in mind, Romeo. She doesn't want you and she's off to Scallop Shores as soon as she can afford it.* Then he'd be back where he'd started, back where he'd chosen to be: alone. Only this time … Lonely.

His cell phone rang, reminding him of looming deadlines and the consequences of procrastination. Paulie. He hadn't spoken to his sister since Wynter had admitted that it was Paulie who'd given her his address. At this point, he wasn't sure whether he should thank her or condemn her.

"I'm on deadline. Whatcha need?" Sam winced. He hadn't meant to come off that rude.

"Everything okay out there at the North Pole?" Always the jokester.

"You mean, has Wynter settled in and are we all cozy, playing house?" Because, yeah, they actually were.

"She had nowhere else to go. I wouldn't have said anything if she didn't absolutely need you."

"I know, sis." It wasn't her fault, or Wynter's even, that his heart was breaking over the fact that Wynter needed him, not for him, but for the roof over his head.

"It's just temporary. And then you get your nice, quiet life back." She actually sounded cheerful.

"Yeah, so everyone keeps telling me," he mumbled.

"Sam? I thought this was what you wanted, to be alone. To be away from everyone that reminded you of that night, of Mom and Dad."

Twelve years ago he would have wholeheartedly agreed. He had wanted to be alone. Well, he'd thought he ought to be alone. Wasn't that the same thing? He'd been punishing himself, pushing everyone he loved away. But now? Wynter showing up on his porch showed him just how much he was missing.

"It was. It is. I don't know. Wynter being here … It's just all being dredged up again, Paulie."

"Have you talked to her about it? Does she know about the nightmares?"

"No! God, no. She tried … She wants to know why I won't go visit you and Gran. She doesn't get it. She just wouldn't understand."

"I think she understands a lot more than you realize, little brother. She's hanging on to her own share of guilt from that night. Were you aware of that?"

"That's crazy. She didn't do anything wrong. She didn't sneak out of the house. She wasn't somewhere she shouldn't have been." Sam's chest ached with unshed tears. He squeezed his eyes shut, gulping in air as he tried to rein in his emotions.

"You didn't do anything wrong either, Sam. In fact, someone was looking out for you that night. Angels, God, whatever you choose to believe in."

"I was in the wrong place at the wrong time." His voice was so gruff he didn't even recognize it.

"You were lucky. You were spared."

"I was supposed to die that night!" Anguish laced his words. He had put off this conversation for twelve years and he certainly didn't want to talk about it now.

"I don't think so." Paulie was quiet for a moment. "There must be a reason Wynter came back into your life. Maybe you're meant to have a second chance."

"Shows what you know. We didn't even have a first chance." Sam was breathing hard, his body trembling with the effort to hold everything inside.

"She needs you, Sam. Her baby needs you."

"You mean Holt's baby? Holt, who was supposed to be my best friend, but I was too busy being a selfish prick and he died?"

"Oh, so you're going to blame yourself for Holt's death, too? Little brother, you are not as all-powerful as you think you are."

He bit his tongue. What he'd been about to say was unforgiveable and couldn't be taken back. His nostrils flared as he blew out a deep breath, struggling to calm his jangled emotions.

"Listen to me, Sammie. It's just the two of you now. Well, nearly three. Take care of them. You need each other."

"She wants to leave. She wants to go back. Eventually she's going to take the baby and go back to Scallop Shores."

"Not if she falls in love with you first."

That one sentence tore him in two. Part of him immediately dismissed the idea as crazy. Wynter could never love someone like him. But part of him, a tiny, hopeful part, fluttered inside his battered, bruised, and broken heart. She needed him now for practical reasons. Was it possible he could get her to need him on an emotional level?

"You never did learn how to stay out of my business, Pauline." He couldn't quite keep the smile out of his voice.

"I love you, too, Sammie."

Chapter 8

"Is the chicken too dry? You aren't eating." Sam's mouth drew down in a frown.

The pain in her back nearly unbearable, Wynter forced a smile. "Not at all. Riley just made a huge batch of chili today. We must have eaten later than I realized."

"He can cook?" Sam's eyebrows disappeared into his hairline.

"Oh, for goodness' sake, he might not be able to walk, but he is still capable of plenty."

"That's not what I meant. Did it taste good?" He pushed his green beans around on his plate. "He's never made a big batch of chili for me."

"Aw, jealous much?" Even the effort to tease was too much. She needed to get away, before Sam realized her discomfort and tried to make a bigger deal of it than it was.

When he'd come over to walk her home, he had alerted both Wynter and Riley to the latest snowstorm that had started without their noticing. Sam had insisted she wait inside while he swept the steps clear of the inch or so of accumulation that had only just begun. The weatherman was now calling for fifteen inches before morning.

If Sam knew her back was hurting this much he would bundle her into the car no matter how much she argued. He'd want her checked out. But it was nothing. Just her body's way of telling her she'd stood up too long or sat on the floor in Riley's spare bedroom with no proper back support. She was paying for not taking enough breaks today.

"Would it destroy your sensitive feelings if I just headed up to bed early tonight?" She threw her friend a lopsided grin that had more to do with pain than pertness.

"If you weren't so pregnant, I'd make you stay to wash the dishes." Sam stuck out his tongue.

"Leave them for morning. Seriously. I'll do them before I leave for Riley's." Now she was hurting *and* feeling guilty.

"I was just teasing. I don't want you standing for longer than necessary."

Amen to that! Wynter struggled to her feet and headed for the door.

"Can I help you up the stairs?"

"Do I look like an invalid?" She knew she'd snapped at him, but she was desperate to get to her room, where he couldn't see the toll the day had taken on her body. She'd never hear the end of it.

"Use my tub again. Soak those muscles."

He knew. Somehow he already knew. And the bitch of it was that she would love to take a bath. But the hot daggers drilling into her back were too distracting to even think of running the water and lowering herself in.

"I'm good, Sam. Just tired." Lumbering up the stairs, she briefly considered stopping halfway for a sit break, but she sensed he was listening for her to get safely to the top.

Finally in her own room, Wynter shut the door and slid to the floor on her knees, curling her back into a stretch to gain some measure of relief. Okay. She'd overdone it. Plenty of rest and she'd be back in the game tomorrow morning. After a few moments, when she'd managed to channel the searing heat into a dull throb, she dressed for bed and was under the covers before the clock struck seven.

Only sleep didn't seem to be part of her future, and Wynter tossed restlessly. Had she pulled a muscle this afternoon? Maybe things were more serious and she'd been too quick to write it off. It was starting to travel to her stomach, great bands of white hot heat, slowly pulling ever tighter. And all the while the snow fell and the roads became more hazardous.

She listened to Sam wash the dishes and then shut himself into his office. Good. He was getting some work done. He'd been spending too much of his valuable work time focused on her and the impending birth. He needed to redirect his energy back to his deadline. Wynter would feel awful if there were repercussions because of her.

A particularly sharp stab stole her breath. What on earth was the matter with her? She still had over two weeks until her due date. This couldn't be it. Deciding she could talk herself into anything if she wanted it badly enough, Wynter pulled the covers up to her chin and tried to concentrate on her happy place.

Because she needed a little more 'happy' right now, she added Sam to the scenario. He was hugging his grandmother and holding little Charlotte. His sister was there too, in the family bookstore on Main Street in Scallop Shores. Paulie's three rowdy boys were chasing each other around the shelves. One big happy family. And since this was her scene, her 'happy' place, it was her family too. Why not? That's what fantasies were all about, right?

Wynter clutched her stomach as another painful spasm ripped through her body. She struggled to keep her breathing under control. A glance at the clock told her two things: it was now two o'clock in the morning and her contractions (because at some point she was forced to call a spade a spade) were now less than five minutes apart. *Stupid, stupid!* She'd waited too long.

With another hot band of steel wrapping all around her body, Wynter had to admit that she was in labor, and things were progressing a little too rapidly. And while she was admitting that scary truth, here was an even more terrifying fact: by giving Sam the chance to work last evening and sleep tonight, the storm had only become worse and they had, more than likely, missed their window to make it to the hospital in time.

When the backache had slithered its way into her stomach, she'd thought it could have been Braxton Hicks. She'd been experiencing them for a week now. She didn't want to be one of those foolish first-time moms who raced to the hospital over every little cramp. The doctor's admonishment at her last appointment rang in her head. *I don't want you two to wait. As soon as those contractions start, give me a call.* And more importantly, *Err on the side of caution.*

Okay, so she hadn't quite trusted what her body had been trying to tell her. But, hey, she'd never done this before! She'd been expecting some grand sign, like her water breaking or being seized by a sudden, debilitating contraction, to start that ball rolling. Things just sort of snuck up on her. She thought she could handle it.

Ohhhh … It was time to get Sam involved. Wynter was through being a martyr. She tossed back the covers and swung her legs off the side of the bed. As her feet searched the floor for her fuzzy slippers, she was blindsided by another contraction. *Too fast! This is happening too fast!* She started to whimper, needing to get to Sam.

Clutching the bedpost, she lurched across the bedroom until she could get a tight hold on the doorframe. She must have looked like a zombie, crawling from doorframe to doorframe until she got to Sam's room. She managed to flip on his light but he didn't even stir. He was so tired. Maybe she should just … *Oh, holy God!* Unable to bear the pain, Wynter crumpled to the floor, letting loose a thin screech as she curled into the fetal position.

"Wyn! What's wrong? Is something the matter with the baby? Are you hurt? Is it …?" He stopped suddenly, realization dawning once he'd had a chance to wake up a little.

"The storm. I waited too long. I wasn't sure. I'm so sorry, Sam," she managed to hiss out.

"It's okay. We can do this. I've been researching home births."

Only Sam. Wynter wanted to laugh at the absurdity of this latest development. Only her Sam would think to cover his bases this way. He probably knew she wouldn't want to inconvenience him. Pain contorted her smile into a grimace. It was nearly constant now, one contraction on top of another. It hurt too much to even cry. Sam's face hovered in front of her, blurry in her pain-filled haze. *Save me. Make this go away.*

He was helping her to the bed when Wynter felt a new rush of humiliation. She knew without asking that Sam had felt her water break. He was standing close enough that she was sure his feet had been splashed. She'd never be able to look him in the eye again. And he hadn't even had to look at her 'down there,' yet.

"Let's get you in bed." He was all efficiency and that helped her ignore her embarrassment long enough to cooperate.

She'd gotten to Sam in time. Everything was going to be all right. Sam would make it all right. "Ahhhh!" The scream startled them both, ripped from between clenched teeth as Wynter bore down on another contraction.

•••

Okay, it was go time. What was the first thing they were supposed to do? Sam looked wildly around the room. He kept his voice calm, and hid the tremors that threatened to rattle his teeth loose. Wynter was counting on him.

He got her into bed and rushed to his desk in the corner. Jerking at the mouse to wake up the screen, he scrolled through bookmarked websites for the one he'd been studying just the night before. He thought he'd have more time.

Yeah, he'd been anticipating this. It was Vermont—in the dead of winter. Chances were pretty damned good that a snowstorm would blow in, making a hospital delivery less and less likely. And he'd been right to assume that Wynter wouldn't take the contractions seriously until it was too late. She was too stubborn for her own good.

So they were doing this. Another scream from the bed had him yanking the power cord from the laptop and carrying it with him back to the other side of the room. The website hadn't bothered to explain that hearing his best friend's gut-wrenching cries of pain would push his own stress levels beyond human endurance.

"Amazing what you can learn from the internet." That ridiculous statement earned him a glare. Yeah, probably best to keep the chatter to a minimum.

"Sam. Call 9-1-1," she panted.

He was going to do that. It was next on his list. Really. He reached for the cell phone that he kept on the nightstand next to his bed. It wasn't there. He stared frantically at the empty charger. Wynter watched him closely, her eyes pleading with him.

"Sam, please!" She clutched at the sheets with a white-knuckled grip, her entire body going rigid. Crap.

"I'll be right back. Don't go anywhere." Sam spun on his heel and raced for the stairs, taking them two at a time, falling on his butt and sliding down the last few. Not letting it stop his momentum, he ran to his office.

Knowing that there was no chance of an ambulance arriving in time for the EMT guys to actually deliver Wynter's baby, Sam could only pray they made it in time to deliver mom and baby to the hospital safely, so they both could be checked out. Sure, babies had been born at home for centuries, before hospitals came into existence, but that didn't mean just anyone could deliver a baby. What if something were to go wrong?

Thank God! His phone was on his desk and the battery was at half strength. Sam put it on speaker and began to explain their situation as soon as the operator came on.

"Can you see the baby? Is it crowning yet?"

"What? No." Geez, he was still in his office! "Wait. I've got to get back upstairs."

Sam flew out of his office and hurried up the stairs, careful not to trip a second time. He stopped at the top of the landing to grab a pile of towels from the linen closet. Wynter's wails were escalating. He wasn't sure what to expect when he burst back into the room.

"Okay, sir. I need you to check if the baby is crowning. Can you do that?"

"Yes. Yes, I can do that." He set the phone down on the mattress, sent Wynter a miserable, apologetic look, and made his way to the foot of the bed.

His bedding was soaked. Wynter's nightgown was sticking to her legs. He would have liked to have pulled it off altogether, so she wouldn't get so chilled, but it seemed only fair to let her retain at least a little of her dignity. He pushed it up over her belly, shoved his own embarrassment down deep and removed her sopping undies. No, this wasn't awkward at all.

"Sir? What can you see?"

My best friend's hoo-hah, Ma'am. And I've got to tell you that this is not how I envisioned seeing it for the first time. Sam swallowed hard and shook his head to clear his thoughts. His eyes widened as he realized what he was seeing.

"Yes! The baby is coming. I see the top of the head."

Embarrassment evaporated, replaced by wonder and excitement. He looked up to find Wynter watching him anxiously. Flashing her a huge grin, he added a thumbs up for good measure. She smiled, shakily.

On a groan she nearly doubled over, grunting as she pushed. Sam's long-abandoned laptop crashed to the floor.

"You need to place your hands on the baby's head now. Don't pull. Just hold them there for support and guide the baby out of the birth canal."

"I have to wash my hands first." He panicked.

"There's no time for that now, sir. You need to place your hands on the baby's head."

Wynter nodded vigorously in agreement.

"Catch her, Sam. Make sure she's safe." She growled it out as she began to push anew.

"Make sure mom is breathing. Can you hear me, ma'am? Pant for me. Pant for your baby."

"Hee hee hee … I'm panting. Tell her I'm panting, Sam."

He couldn't say anything at the moment. His focus was on the perfect little face that had slipped into his waiting hands. She was so warm. Her eyes were scrunched shut. It was happening. Really happening.

"Is the head out yet, sir?"

"Yes, she's out."

"We still need to get those shoulders out. She's not out of the woods yet." The operator spoke matter-of-factly.

Wynter huffed and puffed and moaned through a champion push, in Sam's opinion. He wanted to cheer her on, she was doing so well. Women were so much stronger than men. So much more amazing.

He watched closely, held on firmly and turned the baby just a smidge when he realized it was exactly what was needed to help guide her shoulders out. And then Wynter's little miracle was with them. Sam shouted his exaltation.

"Sir, I need you to gently push the baby's nasal passages to clear them. Is the baby responsive?" A loud wail was all the answer needed.

The 9-1-1 dispatcher talked him through the cutting of the umbilical cord and Sam lifted the newborn up to find that Wynter had disposed of the ruined nightgown and now waited to place the baby to her bosom. He laid her gently against her mother, skin to skin.

"I'm showing that your ambulance is about forty minutes away, at this point. Please remain on the line and I will assist you with the remainder of the delivery."

Sam watched mother and daughter, their bond instantaneous. Tears streamed down Wynter's cheeks, matching his own. Outside the window, pink streaks hinted at morning. It had been one hell of a night. He couldn't get the foolish smile off his face. Charlotte was the most beautiful baby in the world. Born to the most beautiful woman in the world. And Sam realized his life would never be whole unless he found a way to hang on to them both.

Chapter 9

"Go get some rest," she heard whispered in her ear.

She'd dozed off again. Wynter stirred as she felt the baby gently lifted from her bosom. Sam. She blinked, smiling sleepily. She watched as he carried her little bundle to the crib and settled her down for a nap. They'd made it through another long night.

Who knew they would make such a good team? Over the past few days they had fallen into a surprisingly easy routine. They spotted each other for naps while Charlotte was awake. They took turns doing laundry and fixing meals. Not a day went by that Wynter didn't thank God that she had Sam in her life at exactly this moment. The thought of caring for a newborn, alone, sent icy shards down her spine.

It was Sam who showed her how to swaddle Charlotte as tight as a burrito, so she'd sleep better. Sam gave her lessons on diapering. And in a particularly awkward moment, Sam had helped her get the baby to latch on to nurse. Most of that, excluding the breastfeeding part, he'd explained that he picked up that first winter break, home from college, when Paulie's oldest had just come home from the hospital.

The guy was a perfect dad. Only he wasn't really a dad. He wasn't Charlotte's dad. And he wasn't theirs to keep.

Of course, the more she thought of Sam in the role of Charlotte's father, the more guilt she felt over the fact that she wasn't mourning her baby's real father the way he deserved. Holt had wanted this baby so badly. He had bugged her and bugged her to start a family. If only she hadn't put him off for as long as she had. Holt could have had some time with Charlotte before he'd died.

But Wynter hadn't wanted to start a family with a man she'd only settled for. It wasn't fair to either of them, and it wasn't fair to their children. If she could just go back and change the past. She'd been so numb after Sam left, going through the motions of life, not feeling, not caring. Changing the past would mean going back to that night, the night Sam's parents died. The night all their lives had changed forever.

Wynter stood up from the rocker, scuffing out of the nursery like a zombie, past the slumbering child and the man who stood watch over her. She headed downstairs for a cup of herbal tea. It was snowing again. But they had nowhere they needed to be. She slumped against the corner of the counter, holding a mug heavily laden with sugar. If she couldn't have caffeine, she'd find another way to get a little zing in her step.

What would things have been like if Sam's parents had lived? She and Holt and Sam would have attended college together. The Three Musketeers, one for all and all for one. The best of friends. Would they have each found their soul mates? Would it have been awkward to find room in their tight-knit group for girlfriends/ boyfriends? Would they have been happy for each other?

Her back teeth ground together and she frowned into her steaming mug as she thought of Sam with someone else. Who the hell was she to get jealous? He had every right to find someone to love. Still did. Wynter felt physically ill at the thought of Sam meeting Ms. Right, marrying her, and raising his own family.

She needed to get to Scallop Shores. She needed to put some distance between them. The sooner she got over this ridiculous notion of Sam being a replacement father for Charlotte, the better. She was just lonely. That's all.

Sam deserved a woman who could give the man she loved her whole heart. He deserved someone who knew how to treat a man, how to cherish and respect his feelings. He deserved a much better person than her.

"Man, I need some rocket fuel! I have got to get to work if I want to keep this gig." She hadn't even heard him come downstairs.

A strange, gurgling sound came out of Sam's throat. Wynter's head jerked up. He was staring at her chest. His tongue came out to wet his lips, but his eyes remained fixed. He looked … No, she wasn't thinking clearly. Her sleep-deprived brain was making up an attraction that wasn't really there.

She looked down at her chest and nearly died of humiliation. Oh, she was one classy broad, all right! Setting her tea on the counter and acting as nonchalant as she could attempt, Wynter tucked her right breast back into her nightgown. *I'll take 'Most Embarrassing Moment of My Life' for $500, Alex.*

"I should probably get some rest. I seem to be forgetting the basic rules of propriety." Wynter fled to the doorway.

Curiosity got the better of her and she turned to see if her imagination had trumped up that look she thought she'd seen on Sam's face. He was still watching her. His back was so rigid it looked like it hurt. He worked his jaw like that was aching too. His eyes had gone so dark that the little flecks of gold had all but disappeared.

Her breath came in shallow gasps as they eyed each other from a safe distance. Unconsciously, she took a step back, covering her arms over her flimsy nightgown.

"I'm sorry," they spoke over each other.

Wynter blinked.

"Wait. Why are you sorry?"

"I shouldn't have looked. I couldn't stop looking. I … I liked what I saw." Astonishment over his own admission was evident in his expression.

Okay, suspicion confirmed. Wynter opened her mouth to speak, found that words just weren't capable of forming, so she feigned a cough. Feeling as though she ought to acknowledge this confession in some way, she nodded. Sam broke eye contact first, spinning around to focus his attention on the coffee maker. She used that time to escape.

Shutting the door to her bedroom, she pressed her back to it and grinned. This was the most bizarre moment in the history of her adult life. She should be mortified. She should be dreading the next run in with Sam. She should be … anything but giddy. And still she grinned.

Pushing off the door, Wynter rubbed the grainy sleepiness from her eyes. She had to think about this logically. Sam wouldn't normally find her attractive, would he? Heck, she'd just given birth! Changing into a pair of sweats and a flannel shirt, she snorted. *Yeah, she was one sexy catch.*

It had to be the close confines. And the guy must be lonely. He hardly got out, and when he did, it was to visit his acerbic neighbor—who was also a guy. Well, consider her bubble popped. Sam was just happy to have caught sight of a boob, any boob. Wynter sat on the bed to pull on a thick pair of socks. Her sigh may have been a tad melodramatic.

So then the other issue to ponder would be why the thought of Sam finding her attractive made her so happy. She didn't think of Sam like that … Did she? He was her best friend. She was just overly thrilled to have him back in her life again. She was confusing friendliness and gratefulness for him having taken her in, with deeper feelings that had no place in her relationship with Sam.

A knock at her door had her whirling around, patting at her mussed hair and smoothing her wrinkled shirt down. She shook her head, disgusted that she was behaving this way over Sam. It was just Sam. She opened the door, smiling as she realized he looked just as sleepy and rumpled as she did.

"Hey, listen. I just wanted to apologize again. I was a jerk. You're a guest in my house and I was totally inappropriate." He paused, suddenly staring.

"Sam?"

"You're wearing my shirt." She watched his Adam's apple bob up and down. "It looks good on you."

They faced each other from opposite sides of the doorway, the air almost vibrating from the intensity in their gazes. *You take one step closer and I am going to kiss you.* She dug her stocking-covered toes into the deep pile carpet in an effort to keep from throwing herself into Sam's arms. His chest rose and fell, his eyes going from the buttons on the blue plaid to Wynter's lips. He never got up as far as her eyes.

Aw, screw it! She stepped across the threshold and planted one on him. The sound that escaped his mouth seemed an awful lot like relief. Wynter smiled around the kiss. His arms came up around her, his hands briefly cupping her shoulders before pulling her close. He smelled of coffee and some kind of spicy male soap. While she had been the one to initiate the kiss, at some point Sam took over.

His lips nibbled at hers like she was the sweetest fruit, ripe for the picking. She opened for him, marveling at the masterfulness with which he took her mouth. Who knew her Sam was this forceful, this passionate, or this hot? She heard her own voice, a mewl so soft it almost didn't register. No, wait. It was Charlotte. She was waking up.

Sam heard it too, breaking off the kiss and pressing his forehead to hers. Still wrapped in his arms, she savored the moment. Urgent hunger cries began in earnest, across the hall. Wynter slipped out of Sam's grasp, sparing a quick squeeze of his hand before she left.

"I take it back," he said softly.

"Take what back?" She was already across the hall, in the nursery, picking up her newborn.

"My apology. I'm not sorry I ogled you like a stupid teenager. Not if it led to this. This … was not something to be sorry about." With a last, searing look he went back downstairs.

• • •

"Can sleep deprivation make a person horny?"

Sam managed to scrape his chair back in time to avoid being sprayed with coffee … and equal amounts of spit.

"You're *so* cleaning that up, dude. Geez." Riley set his mug down on the kitchen table and swiped the back of a hand across his mouth.

"Yeah, that probably could have come out better."

"Or not at all?" His friend gave him a look that said he'd clearly lost his marbles.

Getting up to retrieve the roll of paper towels from the counter, Sam clenched his jaw and rolled his shoulders. Maybe he was losing it. He was starting to believe that Wynter had feelings for him. Okay, feelings of the shallow, wanna-get-in-your-pants type. But that was a start, right?

He wiped up the mess on the table and the floor, looking up only when he realized how quiet it was. Riley was still watching him carefully. Sam shrugged, getting up off his knees to toss the dirty paper towels. He left the roll on the table in the unfortunate event he should suffer from another case of verbal diarrhea.

"Didn't we already establish that you liked her?" Riley finally broke his silence.

"I'm not talking about me. I'm talking about Wynter."

"She's horny? And you're complaining? What the hell's the matter with you?"

"I'm not complaining." A gusty sigh lifted Sam's bangs as he raised his arms and let them fall loudly into his lap.

"You think you're taking advantage of her 'addled' state?" Riley queried.

"Huh. Hadn't really thought of it that way." Now Sam felt like a heel.

He should have pushed her away the minute she kissed him. She wasn't in her right mind. She was tired and clingy, unaware of what she was doing. He should have turned away and run downstairs. Instead, he'd enjoyed it. Oh, yeah, he'd really enjoyed it. If Charlotte hadn't woken up, he wasn't sure what might have happened.

"Dude, if you could see your face right now." Riley's smirk told him just how pathetic he probably looked.

Yeah, he was hooked.

"*She* kissed *me*. I mean, I would have, I was going to, but she beat me to it."

"Aggressive. Nice." His friend drawled the two words out, making them much more sordid than the situation called for. Sam shot him a dirty look.

"But how do I know it was genuine? I mean, things are pure chaos over there right now." He looked up from his cold cup of coffee. "I shouldn't even be here. She might need me."

"Hold on there, cowboy. Wynter can take care of her own kid for a few minutes while you explain to me what has you so freaked out."

"I'm not freaked out." Sam frowned through the lie. So what if he was.

"She's a beautiful woman with a rack like—" Riley snapped his mouth shut when Sam leaned across the table, his dark eyes menacing. "My point is, she's single, and you're single. Go for it."

"She's my best friend. Who happened to have been married to my other best friend."

"A friend who is no longer in the picture."

"Holt died, Ri. It's not like they got divorced. If he was still alive, Wynter wouldn't even be here."

"And you're sure it was all hearts and roses and cupid stabbing them in the butts with his arrows?"

"It doesn't matter. She belonged to him." Sam slumped down in his chair.

Riley chortled. "Oh, I think Wynter'd kick your ass for that one, boy. She belongs to no one. Of that I am 100 percent certain."

Riley was missing his point. You didn't horn in on a friend's girl. It just wasn't done.

"What happened to taking care of them for Holt? Doing your duty as a friend?"

"That's getting pretty darned hard when I am finding it more and more difficult to think of Wynter as just a friend." Sam sat up in his chair, only to prop his elbows on the table and drop his head into his hands.

"Just do it." His friend pushed.

"Just do what?" Sam mumbled into his cupped hands.

"Have sex with her. Clear the air, so to speak. Get rid of all this tension. You'll feel better. She'll feel better. Well, as long as you don't knock her up again."

"Jesus, Riley, you are so crass!"

"Thanks." The man had the nerve to sit there and grin, proud as could be. Jerk.

"Anyway, I can't." He looked up sadly.

"Oh, enough with this Holt stuff. The guy is gone. His widow needs comforting. Just do it." Again with the Nike slogan. Ugh.

"That's not why." Sam studied his blunt fingernails, refusing to look Riley in the eye.

"You got some kind of erectile dysfunction?" Riley looked equal parts smart-ass and discomfited to be having such a discussion.

"Oh, yeah, thirty years old and I can't get it up." Sam scoffed, rolling his eyes. Until he realized that he'd been incredibly insensitive. Could Riley still … ? Did his disability extend … there? He smacked a palm against his forehead, refusing to even glance at his friend.

"Don't even think it, computer geek! All my man parts are in tip-top working order." Riley glared. "So what is your issue? What's keeping you from jumping her bones?"

Aside from a deep respect for their friendship? Sam sighed.

"I haven't been with a woman … " he broke off, embarrassed to be admitting this to anyone.

"You haven't been with a woman in a while and you're scared of rushing it?" At least Riley had the decency to keep the mocking tone from his voice this time.

"No, you weren't listening. I haven't been with a woman. At all. Ever." Okay, now he really couldn't meet Riley's gaze. *Go ahead, let me have it. Give it your best shot.*

"Holy crap! You're a virgin? How the heck does that even happen?"

Sam scowled. "I wanted Wynter to be my first. I just kind of assumed that when I told her how I felt about her, things would progress and we'd be sleeping together by the end of that summer. Only the telling her part? Yeah, never actually got around to that."

"But you went off to college. You were young, unsupervised. That was your time to let your hair down."

"I was unsupervised anyway, Riley. My parents had just died!" He snapped at his friend.

"Sorry. I didn't mean…"

"No, I'm sorry. I know what you were trying to say." Sam pushed his coffee mug to the center of the table, watching the cooled liquid slosh up against the sides.

"I had strong feelings for Wynter. And apparently stronger morals than I would have ever realized." He pinched the bridge of his nose. "Casual sex with just anyone, for the sake of losing my virginity? Held no interest whatsoever."

"Then you moved to this charming town, where casual sex is no longer even an option," Riley growled.

"Bitter much?"

"Bite me."

"I just figured that when I met the woman I knew I was going to spend the rest of my life with, then I'd be ready."

"Yeah, and she's there, living right under your roof. Go for it." Riley leaned out of his chair, cocking his head to the side. "You scared she's gonna get turned off when she learns you're a virgin?"

"No. Maybe. I dunno. But you're forgetting one thing. Wynter and I have no future. She wants more than I can give her. She wants Scallop Shores and my grandma's old bookstore. She wants to raise Charlotte in her old hometown."

"The hometown you refuse to ever step foot in again."

"Now you're getting it."

"Something's gotta give, dude. Either your morals or your hangups. Otherwise, you're going to explode."

That was the crux of it, wasn't it? He wanted to convince Wynter that they could be happy together—in Vermont. But then he'd be cheating her of her dreams. And if he really loved her, he couldn't do that to her. If he really loved her, he had to let her go. But it sure would make the parting easier if he had some intimate memories to keep with him once she was gone.

Chapter 10

Sam was up to something. He was acting peculiar, and not in that awkward post-first-kiss way. Wynter stretched out on the couch, Charlotte snoozing on her shoulder. Sam was cooking dinner and it smelled delicious. Sweet, with a touch of cinnamon. It smelled more like breakfast to her.

Wynter's favorite meal of the day was breakfast. French toast with extra maple syrup, a tall glass of orange juice, heavy on the pulp, and berries, any kind of berries at all. Her stomach started to rumble. Berries wouldn't be in season for quite a while. More's the pity.

She stroked her daughter's silken head, watching that tiny mouth purse up like she was suckling in her sleep. So precious. So innocent. All the anxiety Wynter had felt about becoming a single mother vanished the moment she held her baby in her arms. She could do this. She was born for this. Yes, they would still make arrangements to move back to Scallop Shores. But she was perfectly content to stay with Sam. As long as she could.

"Want to eat in front of the TV? *Income Property* is coming on." Sam had popped his head around the doorframe, his smile innocent. A little too innocent?

"Why not."

Her favorite breakfast … for dinner. Her favorite show on her favorite cable channel. Wynter eased off the couch, setting the baby in the secondhand bassinet they had found. Touching that soft, warm cheek with her knuckle, she slipped quietly from the living room to the kitchen.

Sam had tucked a dishtowel into the waistband of his jeans. He stood at the stove, flipping French toast on a griddle. A slow, lazy smile stretched across her cheekbones, crinkling the skin around her eyes. Maybe she ought to watch the Food Network. Something about a man cooking her dinner … She licked her lips.

"So what's the occasion? You have to be just as wiped out as I am." Wynter stepped into the kitchen and took a deep sniff, groaning. "I would have been happy with a bowl of cereal."

"What occasion? No occasion. Can't a guy cook dinner without getting grief about it?"

His movements became jerky, agitated. He dropped a piece of battered toast on its way to the griddle. It bounced off the counter and landed on the floor. Sam bit out a four letter word. What was going on here?

"Sam? I wasn't giving you grief. You okay, bud?" The guy wouldn't look her in the eye. Something was definitely up.

"Just go back and sit on the couch. Dinner's almost ready." He stooped to pick up the French toast.

Holding it out in front of him, he added, "I'm not serving this one." As an attempt at humor, it fell flat. His smile looked strained.

Wynter shrugged her shoulders, gave him one last worried once-over and scuffed out of the room in her fuzzy, pink slippers.

Maybe he was regretting their kiss, after all. She pondered that one. Sure, she'd been the one to make the first move, but if he hadn't been looking at her the way he had … She tucked her legs under her as she flopped back down on the couch. Biting her lip, she stared, unseeing, across the room. Now he wouldn't even look at her. What a difference a day made.

"Hope you're hungry. I made enough for an army," Sam trumpeted as he carried a tray loaded down with all her favorites.

"Shh. You'll wake the baby," she admonished.

"Nonsense." He set the tray down and spared a quick look at the infant sleeping a few feet away. "If we start out giving her absolute quiet sleeping conditions, that's what she'll come to expect—to need. Right now they can sleep through anything, and it's best to take advantage of that."

"Honestly—you know way more about parenting newborns than I do." She sighed.

"It's like I explained before. Paulie had her first son while I was home for winter break, my first year of college. You could say I got immersed in a crash course on Newborns 101. Found out I was pretty good at it, actually." He grinned.

She'd forgotten Sam's sister had been pregnant when their parents died. It would have been a few months after Sam had disappeared from her life. Pauline and her husband had lived a few towns over from Scallop Shores. He'd been so close to home.

It was the logical choice, really. If Wynter hadn't been so emotionally shell-shocked, she would have known that. And still she would have stayed away, respected his need for distance.

"I'm glad you didn't push *everyone* away. At least not right away." She spoke gently.

He ignored the comment, setting out the plates and glasses quickly and efficiently. Still he wouldn't look at her. She took a sip of the juice once it was set in front of her. Fresh squeezed. What had she done to deserve this?

"Sam, you made OJ from scratch? Is it my birthday?" She giggled.

"You haven't turned the TV on. You're missing your show." Deftly, he wielded the remote, flipping the television on and turning the channel to a home improvement show featuring a hunky guy that didn't look too much different than Sam. Wynter grinned as she realized the similarity. She knew there was a reason this show was her favorite.

Sam carried his plate to the wingback chair. That was odd. They always sat together. Quizzically, she watched him as he propped his bare feet up on the coffee table and focused his attention on balancing his plate while cutting up his French toast.

"So, I've gotta tell ya. On one hand, I feel like I'm being spoiled. And on the other, I kind of get the feeling I'm being set up for something bigger." She popped a thawed blueberry in her mouth. "Got anything you want to tell me, Sam?"

"Want to? Nope." And to illustrate the point, he stuffed a forkful of food into his mouth, chewing slowly.

"Need to?" She licked syrup off the tip of her finger as she studied her friend.

She was starving, but this whole air of mystery was distracting her. She had to find out what was going on.

"You're missing the show, Wyn. I don't think we've seen this one before."

"I don't give a da—"

"Uh uh uh. Tiny, impressionable ears … " He waggled a finger then gestured toward the bassinet.

Oh, good grief.

"Samuel Dennis, you tell me what is going on. I'm not stupid. Why are you bribing me with French toast?" She watched him squirm in his chair. "What did you do?"

She set the plate down on the coffee table, her appetite having altogether disappeared. Her stomach had begun to twist itself into knots. Her skin felt prickly, right up to her scalp. She rubbed the back of her neck, trying to keep her panic in check. Her gaze flew to the baby, sleeping so peacefully. Suddenly, nothing seemed more important than Charlotte's welfare.

"You were napping. You needed your rest. I was heading past your door and I heard your cell ring. I didn't want it to wake you." He stuffed another bite of food into his mouth and she was forced to wait until he swallowed.

"It was your mom. She was concerned about you. She said you hadn't spoken to her since the day after you got here."

Wynter closed her eyes; her racing heart felt like it was ten times too big to fit inside her chest.

"I thought she ought to know. Her granddaughter had arrived. I sent her a photo from your phone."

"Sam, you had no right." Fat tears rolled down her cheeks. "She doesn't know where you live, though. She can't find us. She can't come get us." She looked up wildly. "Can she?"

"She will never take you back to Florida with them. I promise you that."

"That's not what I asked, Sam." Wynter ground her teeth and tried again. "Can she find us?"

"I invited them to visit." This time she noted he had tears in his eyes. But she'd be damned if it made her any more inclined to forgive him.

"Well, Charlotte, it looks like my dreams of a perfect life for you are over." She spoke to the baby but her eyes glared daggers at Sam.

"Now just stop it right there!" He set his own plate down and stood up, hovering over her angrily.

"I told you I would protect you. I told you they would not take you away from here. Not unless you want to go."

"Why Sam? Why did you do it?"

"Because they have a right to meet her, Wyn. She's their flesh and blood. She's their legacy. They might not have been the best parents in the world. But that doesn't mean they forfeit the right to try to be the best damned grandparents they can possibly be." He was breathing hard.

"This was my choice to make. I wasn't ready for this." Her entire body trembled from fear, from emotion. This was a scenario she hadn't wanted to visit—possibly ever.

"My parents never got to meet Paulie's kids. My mom never got to hold the baby she'd been knitting a whole freaking wardrobe for." He turned away, his shoulders quaking.

She'd been so selfishly absorbed in her own reasons for not wanting her parents to know about Charlotte that Wynter hadn't given any thought to Sam's motives for taking that call. Oh, Sam.

She went to him, pressing herself into his back, resting her cheek against his ratty sweatshirt and wrapping her arms around his chest. His body was rigid. It was taking every ounce of willpower he had not to cry. She knew it.

"We'll figure this out, Sam. We'll let them see her. We'll protect her. Together."

He reached up and grasped one of her hands that rested just over his ribs.

"I'm sorry. I had to do it."

"I know, Sam. I know." Terror unlike anything she had ever known filled Wynter. This was not going to be a pleasant visit. She had to be strong. Attila the Hun and Genghis Khan were coming to town.

• • •

Sam clamped his mouth shut when Wynter pointed out a smudge he'd missed on one of the windows in his office. His office, for crying out loud! Her parents weren't even going to see the inside of this particular room. Why? He swallowed the words he would have liked to utter, their taste bitter on his tongue.

Sam sidestepped just in time to avoid having his toes crushed by an overzealous Wynter wielding the vacuum. He raised his eyes to the ceiling. Was it worth this effort? Would stepping into a spotless home make the couple see their daughter's situation in a different light? Unlikely. But it was something she had to do. And he understood this.

"I'll finish up in here. Why don't you see what we need for groceries? I'll make a quick run before I pick up your folks at the airport," he said, the second she flipped off the vacuum.

"They're renting a car. I got a text this morning. They want to be able to come and go on their own."

"Okay." He drew the word out.

"They're expecting to bring back a car seat, stroller, and a bunch of other baby supplies." Wynter snorted. "Too bad they are spending a fortune on a huge rental for nothing." She yanked the plug from the wall and coiled it around her arm before dragging the vacuum from the room, her spine rigid.

She was still angry with him. And she was tense. Okay, she was beyond tense. He'd love to give her parents the benefit of the doubt, assume they had changed over the years. But watching Wynter prepare for their arrival was really putting a damper on any hope he might have had.

Wynter's brother, Grant, had been a college senior when he and his girlfriend found out they were expecting. He had been planning to go to law school, continue his education. But real life has a way of stepping in and rearranging carefully laid plans. Grant and his girlfriend were thrilled about the baby. But his parents? Not so much.

They'd swooped in, as they were wont to do, issuing orders and telling the parents-to-be exactly what they expected of them. The pregnancy was to be terminated. Grant was to stop seeing his girlfriend, as she was obviously a loose floozy with no morals. She would never be the upstanding woman he needed to support his career and be a model wife. He would continue his schooling and keep up his grades, graduating at the top of his class and earning a spot in one of the most prestigious law firms in the country. They had big plans for their eldest child.

When Grant refused to give in to his parents' demands, they turned to his girlfriend. They offered her money to pay for the abortion and to help set her up, preferably in a different state. Needless to say, she wasn't cooperative. And that's when the Allens resorted to threats.

Apparently, they claimed to have dug up dirt on Grant's poor girlfriend. They threatened to call her out as an unfit mother and take custody of their grandchild. No one really knew if any of their accusations were true, or if they would have been able to gain custody of the child. But Grant and his pregnant girlfriend ran off together.

Sam's frown carved deep creases around his mouth as he remembered how this all went down. Wynter was a junior in high school, at the time. She was getting excellent grades, was beloved by her teachers, her gymnastics coach, everyone who knew her. But when Grant disappeared, Burt and Gloria turned to the only children they had left, and punished them instead.

Wynter and her other brother, Corbin, were pulled from all extracurricular activities. They were to go to school and come straight home. Gloria was a stay-at-home mom who was more than happy to shepherd her children back and forth—the better to know where they were at all times.

That was when Sam first started sneaking into her room. The frown slid off his face. Nothing like a little martial law to make good kids want to break the rules. Well, it wasn't like Wynter turned into a rebel wild-child. She just wanted to spend time with her friends. So she had shown Sam how to climb the twisted oak in the backyard to reach her bedroom. Thank God her parents had never figured this out. He wouldn't have been surprised to find bars on the windows, had they known about his little visits.

In a funny way, he supposed he owed a debt of gratitude to her parents. If it weren't for the ridiculous restrictions they put their children under, Sam and Wynter probably wouldn't have had so much one-on-one time together. She might have gone off shopping and doing whatever it was teenage girls did. Instead, she had asked him to visit. And the two idealistic teens had spent long hours talking about their hopes and dreams.

Shaking the old memories from his head, Sam grabbed his cleaning supplies and left the office. Wynter wasn't downstairs so the baby must have woken up. She'd be in the nursery. He didn't like to interrupt this important bonding time, but her blinding panic was starting to become infectious. He hurried up the stairs, visions of Wynter locked in a bedroom in a fancy Florida condo giving him extra speed.

"We need a plan," he blurted out the moment he reached the doorway to the nursery.

"Ya think?" She arched a copper brow and threw him an exasperated glare. *Yep, she's still angry.*

"They aren't taking you away. And they aren't taking Charlotte. We just need to give them a reason to think that this is the best place for the two of you right now."

"No place is better than theirs. You'd have to be … I don't know." She sighed, sad and defeated.

"Rich? Would that do it?" Excitement raced through his veins as Sam realized they may have a way to overcome this sticky situation.

"You want to lie about your income? That's foolish, Sam."

"I don't want to lie. I want to exploit it." He dropped to his knees in front of the rocker.

"I don't understand." She cocked her head to the side, her eyes squinting.

"Yeah, I live out here in the boonies. My house is modest. But I could just as easily own a mansion." He sat down on the carpet, ducking his head to avoid looking as though he were bragging.

"So … I'm kinda loaded." He chanced a look at Wynter, whose expression was more than a little skeptical. "It's true. The gaming industry is huge. People pay big bucks for high-end software development.

When I balked at the idea of going to work at their company in Palo Alto, they made me an offer."

"An offer you couldn't refuse?" Again with the pointy brow.

"I guess you could say that." His cheeks warmed as he realized that was exactly what it was. "They told me I could work from home. They doubled the offer if I'd just promise to come in once or twice a year to touch base. It's a sweet deal." He shrugged.

"Okay, so you're rich. They aren't greedy. That's not what they're after. I'm still a single mom. They would probably be more inclined to help you get rid of the burden. I'm only here because you are a kind and very generous friend," she reminded him.

Sam pulled up his knees and dropped his chin to one, tapping his leg with restless fingers. She was right. Her parents would probably find that embarrassing. Their daughter was accepting handouts. He chewed on his upper lip, thinking.

"I've got it! They want nothing but the best for you, right? They wanted Grant to have a successful career. If he'd already been a top-notch lawyer when he found out he was going to be a dad, it wouldn't have been an issue."

Wynter shrugged, nodding.

"What if we convince them that we're in a committed relationship? It's probably too soon to announce an engagement, because of Holt." He winced, hoping like hell that he wasn't crossing the line.

"But if they think we're in love, with marriage in the foreseeable future? You would be involved with a successful game developer. Your future would be ensured." He cast a cautious glance at his friend.

"You'd do that for me?" She looked terribly embarrassed.

"I'd do anything for you, you know that." Sam rested a palm on her knee, the awareness that jolted through him an uncomfortable distraction.

"I don't know." She looked pointedly at his hand until he removed it.

"It's just for show. Once they're gone, we go back to the original plan. You save up enough to move back to Scallop Shores." He almost choked on the last few words.

Wynter set the baby on her shoulder and lightly tapped her little back with the heel of her hand.

"It could work. As long as there were no surprise visits." She frowned.

"Your parents don't do anything without a lot of preparation. I don't think spur of the moment trips work for them. They need that element of control. They need to know that you are dropping everything to get ready for their visit."

"Thank you, Sam. You know them so well. You know just how to get us through this." Her grateful smile was his undoing. Sam stood up, his mood turned miserable.

"You're forgetting one thing, Wyn. I'm the one that got us into this mess. Don't thank me for a damned thing. We aren't out of the woods yet."

Disgusted with himself, Sam hung his head and trudged from the room. He had to get groceries for his 'pretend' future in-laws. What had he gotten himself into?

Chapter 11

If the baby continued to be this fussy, Wynter doubted her parents would push very hard to get her to go home with them. Her dad kept finding excuses to drive into town, needing a newspaper, insisting they pick up a new tube of diaper ointment, even making an early morning bagel run. He might as well. They were all awake anyway.

The poor thing had colic. The timing couldn't have been worse, but there was nothing Wynter could do about that. She took perverse pleasure out of the fact that Gloria, who fancied herself the mother of all mothers, could not calm little Charlotte. The one person who seemed to have any soothing effect on the baby at all was Sam.

It was 4am on the third morning of the big visit and Wynter scuffed her way through the downstairs, staying away from the stairwell and trying to give everyone else a chance to sleep. Yeah, maybe if they were sleeping with their pillows over their heads and a few blankets on top of that. The shrill screeches that rent the air were probably enough to be heard at Riley's house. As if he'd ever let her hear the end of that.

She entered the kitchen, lifting her gaze from the scrunched up, beet-red face of her miserable daughter to eye the coffeemaker longingly. Briefly she thought of setting Charlotte in her bouncy seat on the tiled floor while she made a fresh pot of coffee. But Mommy Guilt kept her from indulging her own needs. Lifting the baby to her shoulder, she began the 'shh shh' chant in her ear that occasionally worked to quiet her for a few moments.

"Hey, you look like you could use a break. Give her to me." Sam had snuck into the kitchen, looking all rumpled in his baggy sweats and a T-shirt stretched tight across his torso; his longer hair was sticking up and his jaw was covered in scruffy stubble. Did she say rumpled? She meant sexy.

He wrapped an arm around her shoulders and dropped a kiss on top of her head. Wynter looked up sharply, assuming one of her parents was around. When she realized they were alone in the kitchen she frowned, confused.

"You only have to do that when they're watching, Sam."

"Sorry. You looked like you needed it. I couldn't help myself." His grin was lazy, heavy with the last vestiges of sleep. It made her want to kiss it right off his mouth.

Wynter shook her head to rid it of the images that had no business being there. She transferred Charlotte to Sam's arms, looked at the coffeemaker again and back to Sam. He chuckled, nodding. *Ah, sweet cuppa Joe, come to Momma!*

Sure enough, Mr. Baby Whisperer worked his magic, jiggling Charlotte on his shoulder until her cries turned to hiccups and her hiccups to a blissful snooze. He continued to sway in the center of the kitchen, his head resting against the baby, a content smile on his face.

"How do you do that? It's not fair." Wynter cringed at the petulant tone in her voice. "She's my baby but I can't calm her like you can."

"I don't know. Paulie's oldest had the same problem. Started at about three weeks old and lasted about a month. I was the only one who could get him to sleep."

Wynter peeled a coffee filter from the stack and stuffed it into the basket. She scooped enough grounds in for a full pot and then added one more scoop for good measure. Snapping the filter basket closed, she filled the carafe with water, watching as Sam settled into a chair at the table. He was humming softly. She poured the water into the coffeemaker, set the carafe on the burner and joined her friend at the table. She'd allow herself this one cup.

"I don't know what we'd do without you, Sam." The words held multiple meanings. He could take his pick.

"I'm just lucky I got a chance to have you back in my life." Sam reached across the table with his free hand and clasped one of hers.

Wynter was about to remind him that the affectionate action wasn't necessary when she heard her mother croon from the doorway.

"Look at you lovebirds, sharing a cozy moment." She slipped in and stopped at the table. "Why don't you two run up and get some rest. I'll watch Lottie for a bit." Wynter gritted her teeth at the nickname she'd immediately despised.

As it would be assumed that they were sharing a bed, Wynter had emptied her own room of her belongings and offered it up to her parents as the guest bedroom.

Wynter was sharing Sam's room, sure, but by no means were they really sharing the bed. In reality, they took turns, one sleeping in the bed and one camping out on the floor. Sam had tried to insist Wynter use the bed every night, but she wouldn't hear of it. They locked the door so her parents couldn't sneak in and catch them in their ruse. If it looked like they wanted their privacy, so much the better.

"Uh uh. Too much at stake. I started that pot of coffee, I get to have one amazing cup of it," Wynter said with an emphatic nod.

"Suit yourself." Her mother bustled into the kitchen-proper, opening the fridge and taking out ingredients for breakfast.

"Mom, you don't have to cook. Just sit with us for a minute. It's quiet. Let's enjoy it."

Gloria peered around the open door of a cabinet as she took out a mixing bowl. Her eyes settled on Sam, who looked quite content to hold his precious charge.

"I'm up. I might as well be useful." She cracked a few eggs into the bowl and began to whisk.

The coffeemaker burbled a last gasp, signaling the end of the brew cycle. Wynter licked her lips. How long had it been since she'd indulged in a little caffeine? She poured a cup of coffee then held up an empty mug for Sam, who shook his head. She shrugged her shoulders, gliding to the fridge for some creamer before she settled in at the table with her new little family.

"You know, it's funny, Sam. When you all were in high school, Wynnie's father and I would have sworn you and Holt were a couple." Gloria waved the wooden spatula jauntily in the air.

Did the woman not have a filter? Wynter shot an apologetic glance at Sam over the brim of her cup. He held her look for a moment, a slight smile tugging at the corners of his mouth.

It was what they had wanted them to think. Gloria and Burt wouldn't see the boys as a threat to their only daughter's future if they thought they were gay. This was, perhaps, the reason Sam and Holt had grudgingly been allowed to come over after school to do homework, occasionally staying for dinner.

Wynter was afraid they played it up a little too well at times, but oh how they had laughed about it afterwards when they'd snuck back later up the tree into her room. Her smile was melancholy, as she thought back to a time when she'd still had both Sam and Holt in her life.

"Now here she is taking up with not one, but both of you." Gloria chattered on, heedless of the insensitivity in her words.

"A little respect, Mother?" Wynter gritted her teeth.

"What's the matter?" The woman smiled cheerily from the stove. "Oh, you mean because you chose Sam as second runner up?"

"No, she meant show a little respect for Holt. He's been gone less than a year." Sam's eyes flashed a warning that even Gloria seemed to have no trouble interpreting.

"I wonder, though, what Holt's parents would think of this latest development. Their precious, only child, being replaced so quickly … and by someone he used to be so close to."

Guilt weighed down so heavily, it was a wonder Wynter's chair didn't break. She couldn't look at her mother, didn't dare see the look on Sam's face. She stared morosely into the cup of coffee that now held all the appeal of a puddle of mud.

"They would want me to be happy, I'm sure." *Was she?* "Their granddaughter deserves a father figure in her life. Why not someone they know and already approve of?"

Wynter's mother went back to scrambling eggs, without another comment. Apparently she'd run out of snarky things to say. The two young people sat at the table, watching the baby sleep.

The knot of anxiousness that had wound itself around her heart the minute Sam told her about his phone conversation with her parents began to ease. She'd get through this. Dare she hope that her friend was right? Her parents just wanted to secure a spot for themselves in their granddaughter's life? They would visit for a few days and leave, knowing that their girls were well taken care of? *Oh, please.* She could dream though, right?

• • •

Mother Nature had dumped a few more inches of the white stuff overnight. It was now close to March and Sam was finding it difficult to remember what his yard looked like beneath this snowy mantle. Green? The only green around right now were the green garbage cans that he'd just set out at the end of the driveway. Muttering under his breath, he put his back into the chore, clearing the porch steps.

Wynter's parents had been visiting for a week. They hadn't offered up any sort of time frame on how long they planned to stay. Neither had they officially stated that they intended to bring Wyn and Charlotte back to Florida with them. So he bided his time. And bit his tongue. Oh, he'd bitten his tongue down to a stub. But it was his fault they were here, after all.

He rather enjoyed performing the 'couple' routine with Wynter. He was free to act on his feelings. Any excuse to take her hand in his, rub her back as they stood side by side, or brush a kiss against her temple while they cuddled on the couch, watching TV. But the nights? The nights were torture.

He'd give anything to share a bed with Wynter. It wasn't even about the sex, though his heartbeat sped up just thinking about her lying there, scantily clad and drowsy. It might mean turning in his man card if he had to voice it aloud, but Sam would have been happy to just hold her. To wrap his arms around her, press his nose into her sweetly scented hair and let the rhythm of her breathing lull him to sleep.

But she didn't feel the same way. Wynter kept her distance. She clutched at the neckline of her robe, whenever they were alone in his room. She snuck under the covers before she removed it. She peeked at him beneath her lashes, her expression awkward, uncomfortable, even. He wanted desperately to believe that it was the stress of her parents' visit that was causing her to pull away from him. It was like their kiss had never happened.

Sam finished clearing off the bottom step and started on the driveway. The front door creaked open but he didn't bother to turn around. He continued to shovel, his stiff shoulders making the movements jerky. He wasn't in the mood for company. Eventually he heard footsteps shuffling toward him.

"This isn't where I pictured her." Gloria thumped down the steps to block Sam's path.

"She won't go to Florida with you." It wasn't his place to have this particular conversation, but the words came out, unbidden.

"She's flighty. She doesn't know what she wants."

"Maybe you just haven't been listening. Because it's pretty darned clear to me." Sam speared the shovel into the middle of a snow covered hydrangea bush. The handle quivered for a moment then held fast.

"Wynter wants to raise her baby in Scallop Shores. She wants to go home." She'd kill him for admitting that.

"So this whole scenario is temporary? See? She's flighty."

"I didn't say she'd be going alone." Oh God. Could he pull off this whopper? "When we're ready, we'll all go."

"You'd go back to Scallop Shores? Where your parents died?" He saw the determined glint in Gloria's eyes. She was baiting him.

"My sister has moved back there and my grandmother still lives there."

"Yes, but I heard you haven't been back since that night. Now, all of a sudden, you're going to set up house in the one place you've been hiding from your whole adult life?"

If the woman was smart, she wouldn't try so hard to alienate the one person who had made a visit with her granddaughter possible. Did she know how to be kind to anyone? The loving and nurturing gene must have skipped a generation with her.

"So I've noticed you still haven't asked for a copy of my bank statement. Can we just assume you think I have the financial means to take care of your daughter?"

"You certainly wouldn't know it by looking at this house." She sniffed disdainfully, raising her nose in the air as she took in Sam's home.

"Bottom line, Gloria? It's cold out here and I'd like to finish up this driveway before lunch." Sam jerked the shovel out of the flower bush and turned away from the woman, getting back to work.

"That foolish Holt took her away from me. They didn't have the money to visit. I offered him money. I offered him money before they even got married. He wouldn't take it." She pursed her lips, pacing a bit before adding, "I don't like her being out here in the middle of nowhere. My daughter needs more than … this." She waved her hands around, her expression one of distaste.

"Moving back to Scallop Shores is not going to get Wynter any closer to you in Florida." He pitched a shovelful of snow just over Gloria's shoulder, hiding a smile as she jumped.

"I don't want my Wynnie to keep running from me. I want to see my granddaughter grow up."

"Then stop trying to control her. You already pushed one child out of your life. Grant's kids don't know their grandparents because of you." Sam watched her eyes widen in anger, an old pain lingering just below the surface.

"You don't know your place, young man!"

"This *is* my place. And while you're staying at *my* place, you will treat Wynter with the respect she deserves. She is an amazing woman and a phenomenal mother. She is doing the best she can for that little girl. She has big plans for Charlotte and it's up to you whether you find yourself a part of those plans or not."

"You love her then." It wasn't a question.

They stared each other down.

"Fine. Move back to Scallop Shores. Maybe her father and I will move back too."

Wynter would have a heart attack if she heard her mother announce that. But Sam knew it for the bluff that it was.

"You're welcome to visit us any time." His unspoken conditions hung in the air between them.

"Florida seems like much more of a vacation destination, in my opinion. And since you claim to have all this money … "

Ever the control freak. Sam lowered his gaze to the ground, before she could see him rolling his eyes. He tried to keep in mind that having a mother like Gloria was better than having no mother at all. The smile he pinned to his face hurt, as though he'd used actual thumbtacks to attach it.

"I'm sure I could talk her into the occasional sunny trip down south."

"That's a good boy." Gloria climbed up one step then turned and spoke over her shoulder. "I'm making my beef stew tonight. Bring your appetite."

Sam clenched his jaw, tightening his muscles to keep the shudder from jarring loose. He nodded through the stiff smile and prayed she'd hurry back into the house. Gloria's stew was famous—for being revolting! Sam and Holt had suffered through batches of the stuff because it meant spending time with Wynter. Good God, how much longer was this woman going to be under his roof?

Gloria tramped up the stairs and opened the door, knocking the snow from her boots before she entered.

"I'll make a double batch so you two won't have to cook for a while, after we're gone. Burt got us a flight out tomorrow afternoon." She tossed back before she shut the door firmly behind her.

"Thank you." He spoke to the closed door. *Thank you for getting the hell out of my house.*

Sam finished the driveway in record time. Knowing there was a light at the end of the tunnel gave him wings. He whistled as he worked, looking forward to getting his little family back to himself. Just Wynter and Charlotte and him, alone in the house again.

Only he'd promised he would move them to Scallop Shores. The tune he'd been whistling ended on a flat note. He had lied to Gloria. He couldn't go back. Even if that was the only way he could hold on to Wynter, to his temporary family. There were too many memories, too much pain left behind in Scallop Shores. He had to let her go, eventually. He put away the shovel, heading back for the house. The clock that ticked down the time he had left with Wynter and the baby sounding ominously loud in the still, pre-spring morning.

Chapter 12

"I'd rethink that second brownie if I were you, Wynnie. Sam's not going to want you if you let yourself go just because you've had a baby."

Picturing the light at the end of the tunnel that was her parents' departure, Wynter smiled brightly. Making sure to catch her mother's eye, she added a dollop of ice cream to the top of the brownie and spooned up a big bite. Ignoring her mother's hands on her hips and the 'I'm-telling-you-you'll-regret-it' raise of her eyebrows, she focused instead on the mix of cold ice cream with the warm brownie, the melted chocolate chips sliding down her throat after coating her tongue with blissful sweetness.

Sam caught her eye across the table and winked. It brought back memories of growing up under Gloria's thumb. Sam—and Holt as well—had made it so much more tolerable. On the one hand, she was happy, grateful she had Sam to lend support. But on the other she was frustrated that her mother could make her feel like a recalcitrant child. She was an adult, with an infant of her own, for goodness' sake! She had to stop letting Gloria get under her skin. Enough was enough.

"So, when is the wedding?" Gloria looked from Wynter to Sam. The smug smirk peeling the corners of her mouth upward showed how pleased she was that she had managed to rattle her daughter's cage … Again.

"Mother!"

Wynter sent a horrified look at Sam, amazed when he didn't seem nearly as uncomfortable about the turn of conversation as she was. Gloria wasn't his mother. She couldn't push his buttons as easily as she could her daughter's.

"And do you intend to invite your brother? Because I don't think it's appropriate for him to attend when he hasn't participated in being a member of this family for so long."

"A wedding comes after a proposal, mother. A proposal comes after a good long courtship."

"Oh, please. No one says courtship anymore. You've got a baby to think about now. If Sam is going to raise Lottie as his own, you need to move forward."

"Sam, I want to apologize for my mother. Her conversationally-appropriate filter seems to be broken." When mortified, resort to humor.

"My daughter will not just shack up with a guy because it's convenient." Burt's voice thundered across the table. Oh, good Lord! Charlotte whimpered in her sleep, from the bassinette in the adjoining room.

"She didn't say we *wouldn't* get married, Mr. Allen. We just don't see the need to rush. I love your daughter, sir. And I love little Charlotte. I intend to take care of both of them for the rest of my life."

Wynter stood up from the table, ostensibly to check on her sleeping baby. She felt like a weasel, forcing Sam to lie to her parents. She didn't feel bad lying to them. No, they had brought this all on themselves. But poor Sam was having to go above and beyond the call of even the closest friendship. This is not what she'd meant to ask of him when she showed up on his doorstep, pregnant, broke, and incredibly desperate.

When she returned from the living room, assured that the livelier-than-necessary conversation hadn't woken Charlotte, her father had settled down. He was tucking into his third helping of dessert, not that her mother chose to point that out. Gloria's smile, upon seeing Wynter in the doorway, was calculating. She wasn't finished yet.

"So when do you think you'll be moving back to Scallop Shores?" And there it was.

She stopped breathing. Did Gloria know this whole thing was a farce? The woman's sharp gray eyes pinned her to the spot. Wynter's brain shorted out. She couldn't form words, just stood there with her mouth slightly open. Burt turned in his seat, also awaiting a response.

"We haven't discussed the specifics, have we, babe? It'd be best if we waited until spring, when the snow finally melts and we can think about putting the house on the market."

Oh, Sam. One lie just led to another. She'd really gotten him into a pickle.

"Mom, I promise we aren't going to make any life-altering changes without giving you plenty of notice. Okay?"

"You mean like searching out a friend you hadn't seen in over ten years, in favor of moving in with your parents when you were nearly ready to give birth?"

"Sure beats being completely shut out of your son's life, and the lives of his children, though, because your control-freak ways pushed him away, doesn't it?" That's right. She went there.

Gloria's face turned red, then slightly purple. Her eyes went from wide to a scrunched up mean. Her mouth opened, closed, the tight seal of her lips wrinkling like she'd been sucking on lemons. She whipped around, her focus now on Burt, urging him to get involved. He started to speak and Wynter cut him off.

"No, you both listen to me. If you want any kind of relationship with me or with Charlotte, you will stop with the smothering." She stepped away from the doorframe, pointing a finger at her mother and then swinging it to include her father.

"You need to trust that I am a grown woman who can take care of herself. It isn't Sam's responsibility to take care of me. If he chooses to be a part of our little family, it's because he wants to, not because he has to."

Wynter suddenly realized her speech was really meant for him. She could care less whether her parents understood her need to be independent. But Sam? She didn't want his charity. She didn't want him to feel obligated to take care of her and her daughter.

She snuck a glance at him across the table. Even his eyes were smiling, and his expression bolstered her flagging confidence. What she wouldn't give for this scenario to be real. That they really were headed for marriage. That Sam was finally willing to move back to Scallop Shores, to face his demons. He looked at her with such warmth, such affection. It was almost like—No. She had to remember they were putting on an act for the benefit of her parents. Her imagination was sending her down a path she had no business following.

• • •

This was the last night they would have to share a bedroom under the guise that they were a loving couple. Wynter should have felt relieved. Instead, she found herself following him with her eyes, watching him shuck his jeans to sleep in his boxers, wishing she had the nerve to invite him to share the bed.

Sam turned, as though he could feel her eyes upon him. He frowned. She schooled her features to hide her own turmoil, as he seemed to understand that something was up. She experimented with a shaky smile. His frown deepened. Hey, it had been a long day. As far as acting went, she was spent. He propped a pillow and lay down on top of the covers with her, thankfully leaving his T-shirt on.

"You feeling guilty for lying to your parents?"

"Not at all. They deserve it." She didn't even blink. "I'm feeling guilty that *you* had to lie. This can't be easy for you."

"I don't know. I'm kind of surprised at how good I am. Should I be worried? Are you a bad influence on me?"

Wynter giggled, punching her friend in the arm before settling down to rest her head on his chest. This should have put her at ease. They'd snuggled like this so often in the past. Sam would climb the old oak and tap on her window. She'd let him in and they would talk the night away. He'd comb his fingers through her hair. It had always made her want to purr. Eventually, she'd fall asleep. Sam would let himself out the window, closing it as best he could, before sneaking back into his own house in the wee hours of the morning. Her parents had been none the wiser.

Sam was on the scrawny side in high school, his slight chest bony, his long arms skinny. While they had been apart he had changed. Her skinny computer nerd had filled out. Now her head rested on one well-defined pec, while her arm stretched across the wide expanse of his chest. He was her Sam, and then some. Instead of snuggling into his chest, ready to chat the night away, Wynter found herself distracted by the scent of his spicy soap. Her fingers itched to play with the hair that curled against his neck. She remained still, hoping the steady thrum of his heartbeat beneath her cheek would calm her heightened senses.

"I was proud of you tonight, standing up to your parents like you did." His deep voice rumbled through his chest, sending shivers all the way to her curling toes.

Great. Now she just wanted to crawl up his body and whisper naughty things in his ear. Wynter stiffened against Sam's side. What used to be as natural as breathing was now the sweetest form of torture. Every place their bodies touched tingled. Her skin wanted more surface area covered. Her brain wanted her to lift off and hover, removing herself from the temptation that was her scrumptious best friend.

"I'll just be glad when they leave." Wynter couldn't resist rubbing her cheek against the worn fabric of Sam's tee. His fingertips skittered up her arm before finding their way into her hair to massage her scalp.

"Mmm … Me too." The gravelly tone of Sam's voice caught her off guard. Had he meant that the way it sounded? Or were her own needs interpreting that as suggestive?

The pads of his fingers pressed little circles into her hairline. Wynter ground her teeth together, suppressing the moan that would betray exactly how she really felt about him struggling to escape.

"Sam, about Scallop Shores. You didn't have to tell my parents you would come with me. I understand why you stay away." Understood but hated it.

He used the pressure from his fingertips in her hair to force her to meet his eyes. His jaw was rigid, his eyes dark and dangerous. She opened her mouth to speak but it hung slack as she registered the hunger in his expression.

"I don't want to talk about Scallop Shores."

"But—" *Shut me up, Sam.*

And he did. Sam hauled her up, bringing their faces into alignment before claiming her lips in a kiss that stole every breath, every thought, every last reservation she had. This time the moan did escape, slipping from her mouth into his. He swallowed it greedily, sharing a low sonorous growl of his own.

She wanted more. Her fingers became restless, darting over surfaces she hadn't ever imagined touching. This was her Sam, after all, and she didn't think of her Sam like *that*. Except that now she couldn't stop thinking of Sam and sex in the same context. He made her want things she couldn't have. He made her bold, ready to ask for what she needed.

His large hands cupped her bottom, pulling her against him right where the tightest bundle of nerves scraped against hard steel, urging her to lose all control and ride this wanton wave of lust to the finish. She couldn't think. She could only need. Her body trembled with the force of it.

Then the toilet flushed in the hallway and her father exited the bathroom, whistling a tune. She knew, from memory, that he carried a rolled up magazine under his arm. Squeezing her eyes shut, she broke the kiss, trying to gain control of the situation. Sam held her chin up with one finger, and when she peeked through her lashes, she saw that he had no intention of letting her father interrupt what they had started.

She buried her face in his chest. This had gotten completely out of control. Never mind that it was what she wanted more than anything in the world. It was wrong. She couldn't have Sam. She shouldn't have Sam. Kissing Sam, touching Sam, it was all so good. And that was what made it wrong.

Wynter pushed herself off his chest and scrambled for the edge of the bed, shrugging off his hand when he reached for her shoulder. *God, he's going to think I'm nuts!* How to explain the guilt, the wrongness of wanting her best friend? She'd been married to Holt for nearly ten years and had never felt this passion, this all-consuming desperation to share herself with him. This was wrong.

Really, what kind of woman throws herself into the arms of another man mere months after losing her husband, the father of her new baby girl? A woman who should never have married that man in the first place. Holt had been there for her at a time when she'd felt alone, lost. He'd deserved a wife who gave him her whole body and heart. He just hadn't gotten it.

And now she was giving herself to Sam with all the reckless abandon of a … She couldn't even think the word. It was dirty. It was shameful. Yet it fit her to a T. *Please forgive me, Holt. I'm acting like a slut.* There. She'd said it, at least in her own head. Admitting it didn't make the reality of it feel any better.

"Talk to me, Wyn. I'm not going anywhere." This time he cupped both shoulders tightly, pulling her against him.

"See, that's just the thing. You aren't going anywhere. But I am." She turned, catching sight of his stubbled jaw and resisting the urge to reach out and stroke it with her fingertips.

"My future is in Scallop Shores. I've known that I would go back since Holt and I left for college. As much as I want you in my life, in Charlotte's life, it's just not going to work. Unless you're willing to face your past, slay your demons, this," she laid a palm on his chest and then moved it to her own, "this is just temporary. And I don't want to start something with you that we can't finish."

His silence told her he understood, and agreed. What had she been expecting? That he'd suddenly offer to overlook a past that had haunted him for twelve years? His focus was on her left shoulder and try as she might, Wynter could not get him to look her in the eye. His expression was pained. She hadn't meant to make him feel guilty. That was all on him.

"It's late, Sam. Let's get some sleep."

This time he did look up, and the raw vulnerability she witnessed made Wynter want to take his hand and help him beneath the covers. She yearned to hold him, kiss him and tell him everything was going to be okay.

It was supposed to be all about her. Now that Holt was gone, it was Wynter's chance to live independently, make her own choices. She had her daughter to think of and no time for complications.

But the more time she spent with Sam, the tighter he became woven into her life. They'd shared a past, they were connected. She'd understood that, had shamefully tried to exploit that. But these new feelings she was having for Sam? It was getting harder and harder to separate her wants and needs, her goals for the future from this old farmhouse in Middle-Of-Nowhere Vermont, or from the man who used to be her buddy and was starting to look an awful lot like her soul mate, a concept she'd considered a fairy tale until very recently.

Wynter slipped beneath the covers alone. Her toes stretched across the length of the mattress as though, if she stretched far enough, she could reach Sam, curled up with an extra blanket on the floor beside the closet. She hugged the pillow, catching just a lingering trace of Sam's scent. Burying her face, she breathed deep. If she'd thought her life was complicated before arriving at Sam's place, it was nothing compared to now.

• • •

The cement floor of the basement was chilly, even under her stocking feet. Wynter did a little dance to warm up, as she scooped the warm clothes from the dryer into the laundry basket at her feet. Kicking it aside, she transferred the wet things from the washing machine into the dryer and turned it back on.

"Were you just going to hide down here until we left?" The sound of the dryer had masked her mother's arrival.

She'd been planning to come back upstairs. Maybe at the last possible second, but she'd have been there to see them off. Barely. Slipping into her dutiful daughter persona, Wynter conjured a mental clock, ticking down the minutes until her mother was in that large rental currently parked in the driveway, heading toward the airport and away from them.

"Just getting a little laundry done while Charlotte sleeps." She didn't have the energy for another go 'round.

Hauling the basket up on her hip, she was about to lead the way back up to the living room when her mother stopped her with a hand on her arm. Gloria wasn't the touchy-feely type, so this was enough to stop Wynter in her tracks.

"I wanted to talk to you alone. Before we go."

Yep. Another go 'round.

"Mom, I'm tired and I'm busy. You remember what it was like having a newborn around, I'm sure. There is very little time to get things done in between Charlotte's little catnaps."

"I do, yes. I've been thinking about that a lot, actually."

Dropping her arm to her side, Gloria seemed to struggle for the right words.

This was interesting. Wynter set the basket of clothes on the dryer and began pairing socks, holding them together and rolling them into a ball, just as her mother had taught her.

"We haven't had the easiest relationship. I know I'm partly to blame for that.

Before she could cough, sputter, gag, or in any other way acknowledge that gross exaggeration of the truth, her mother had continued.

"Everything I did was out of love for you and your brothers. I was the best mother I knew how to be. I want you to know how much I loved you all, how much I still love you."

"Mom, I don't know what you want me to say."

She'd run out of socks and was frantically searching the bottom of the basket for anything that would keep her from having to make eye contact. Who was this alien pod person that had taken over her mother's body? The lonely little girl that had craved her mother's affection was still there, hiding inside Wynter's heart. And she was intrigued.

The adult in her was suspicious. Why now? Was this a last-minute ploy to get her to see reason and get her to fly home to Florida with them?

"I bought something, just a little present."

Ah, there we go! A plane ticket, no doubt.

"Mom, you didn't have to. Really."

Gloria reached into the pocket of her baggy brown corduroys and withdrew a small box. It was too tiny to house a plane ticket. She held it out to Wynter, her expression one of uncertainty.

Taking a deep breath, her nose picking out equal parts dryer sheet and musty basement, Wynter accepted the box with trepidation. Her mother watched her closely. It was unnerving, really. A simple white box, it made very little sound when she shook it.

Removing the lid, she gasped. Inside was a bracelet, clearly meant for an infant. The links were gold, delicate. Dangling from the center of the chain was a flat charm, a filigreed rose etched into the metal.

"It's beautiful."

"Turn it over." Gloria gestured with her hand.

Engraved on the back were the words *Beloved Granddaughter*. Wynter pressed her fingers to her mouth. Emotions she didn't think she possessed for the woman in front of her clogged her throat, made it impossible to speak.

"She doesn't have to wear it, of course. I just thought she ought to have something to remember us by."

"Remember you by? It's not like this is the last time you'll ever see her."

"Isn't it? You've made it more than clear that you don't need us."

"I just … you were pushing too hard. I guess I was a little unreasonable."

Wynter wrapped her arms around her mother. The slight woman felt stiff. They stood awkwardly for a few moments. Nope. Affection just didn't seem to come naturally with them. The relief was tangible when they pulled apart.

"Thank you. I will make sure Charlotte treasures this bracelet."

Gloria offered her a quiet smile and patted her hand. "There's something in the bottom of the box for you, too. But you can look at it later, after we're gone." Then she retreated up the stairs, leaving Wynter stunned.

Had she misjudged her mother? Perhaps the idea of losing the relationship of another grandchild had made the woman resolve to be a better person. It didn't erase the years of childhood trauma Gloria had inflicted on Wynter, but it was a start. A fresh start. And that made her heart feel good.

They made it through the rest of the morning and her parents' departure rather uneventfully. It wasn't until hours later that she recalled her mother's mention of a gift and picked up the jewelry box again. There was a piece of paper stuck inside the bottom, underneath the soft batting. Curiosity piquing, Wynter plucked it out and unfolded it.

A check made out to her in the amount of ten thousand dollars was pinched between her trembling fingers. In the subject line, at the bottom of the check, it read Scallop Shores Travel Fund.

Of course. It was just like her parents to throw money at a problem. Her mother had called it a gift, but there were so many different ways she could interpret this check. Did they really just want to help? Or was this a means to get in one last dig at Wynter, to say that they didn't think she could carve out a new life for her daughter without their assistance or Sam's?

Stiffening her spine, she tore up the check, until the pieces of paper were so tiny she couldn't make out any of the writing. Wynter would earn her own way back to Scallop Shores. She would find a way to pay back Sam for his generosity. And she'd do it on her own.

Chapter 13

"I don't understand why you can't just keep everything the way it is. Convince Wynter that she wants to be with you, and it doesn't matter where the two of you live." Riley never looked up from the staring contest he was having with little Charlotte.

"So then I get everything I've always wanted and to hell with her dreams?" Sam scoffed.

"Shh. Daddy doesn't need to start teaching you this colorful new language just yet, does he Charlotte? He's just whiny because he's not getting any. It's what we call 'sexually frustrated'. But you have a few years before we need to explain where you came from."

"Yeah, like, not from me. I'm not her daddy, Ri. Cut it out."

"It may not have been your sperm that helped give her life, but that doesn't matter. You're the man in her life right now. Well, you and her coolest uncle in the world. Uncle Riley." He chucked the baby under her chin.

Sam rolled his eyes.

"You're completely glossing over Holt's role in all of this. Wynter loved the guy enough to marry him, to have his baby. She's still grieving."

"Uh huh. So then why is she choosing to suck face with you?" Riley puckered up his lips, making kissing noises at Charlotte.

Sam threw his hands up in the air and stalked to the window. He knew he shouldn't have revealed that little tidbit to Riley. The man was worse than a gossiping old granny. He gritted his teeth and rested his hands on the window frame. Riley hadn't stopped cooing at the baby.

Mother Nature had decided to be kind, bestowing a string of warm days to mark the end of winter and the start of spring. But to the people of Braeden, that meant rapid snow melt, slush, basement flooding, and mud. Lots of mud. Yeah, he had so much to offer Wynter here.

Sam tried to remember what it had been like in Scallop Shores at the beginning of spring. It was only a four hour drive northeast. Surely the conditions couldn't be that different. He knew he held his old hometown to a higher standard, kept it postcard-perfect in his memory. He'd decided a long time ago that he was never going back. Sam had lost the right to live in Scallop Shores the night he'd let his parents die without him.

"Yo, Sammy, someone is smelling a little funky over here."

"So take a shower." He allowed a smile to slide over his features before turning away from the window.

"Aw, and here I was going to offer to change her." Riley held the baby out to Sam with a wink and a wicked grin.

"You wouldn't know which end of a baby to diaper if you had to. Come here, Charlotte, Sam will clean you right up."

He carried the baby to the couch, cradling her in one arm while using the other to arrange the changing pad and supplies he'd need. Riley rolled his chair closer. Sam started to unswaddle the infant, knowing, before he was done, that he was dealing with a full blow out.

"Seriously! How can someone so incredibly cute do something so horribly revolting?" Riley covered his eyes in horror, waving an arm like he was warding off a major evil.

"Babies poop, Ri. It's what they do. They eat. They sleep. They poop. Not much else at this point." His movements were efficient. The mess didn't bother him at all.

"You were so born for this."

"To get attached to a little girl and her mother when I know they're going to leave me?"

"No, idiot! To be a dad. You make it look effortless. You kind of make me wonder what it would be like to take on that kind of responsibility. If I could get past the fact that I can't run with my kids, teach them to walk, or ride a bike. You can do all that. And you should."

Sam released a long sigh. "This life … This moment, it's not supposed to be mine. It was supposed to be Holt's. I feel like I'm stealing something from him, you know?"

"You didn't kill him, Sam. He was gone before you even found out about Charlotte. Besides, he would want you to step up. Friends do that for each other."

"Yeah, and friends support each other's dreams. Which is why I have to let Wynter go. She wants to live in Scallop Shores. She wants to run my grandmother's book store."

"What if your grandmother doesn't want her to run it? She's *your* grandma. Tell her you want Wynter to stay with you. Have her convince Wynter that she should find a new dream."

"See? This is why you're single." Sam stuffed the soiled baby clothes in a plastic bag to be washed later. He tossed the dirty diaper, wrapped tightly in another plastic bag, onto Riley's lap. "Be a pal and get rid of that, would ya?"

"I'm just saying, you've spent the last twelve years pining for this woman. Now you've got her back. Things are good. They'd be better if you were actually sleeping together, but they're good. Hang on to that." He rolled off to throw away the garbage.

Sam smiled sadly at the tiny baby he was dressing. She held his gaze, yawning huge. He had to get her back to the house so Wynter could feed her before her nap. He stood up and went looking for Riley, placing Charlotte in his arms so he could wash his hands.

"My conscience won't let me hold on to her. I don't expect you to understand that."

"So you're saying I don't have a conscience? Dude, that's cold." Riley's tone suggested he wasn't actually angry, so perhaps he did understand more than Sam realized.

"I wish there was a plan C. We could move to a small town, something on the coast that reminded Wynter of Scallop Shores. We could get her that book store she wants. I can design software anywhere." He stared, unseeing, across the room. His imagination started to create a life for the three of them, a life that didn't involve past mistakes, years of separation or a mountain of guilt.

"I've always liked the seashore. Too bad wheelchairs don't work too well on sand."

"Oh, quit your whining, Nancy. You know you're coming with us." Sam focused his gaze on his friend. Okay, so a Plan C was sounding pretty sweet.

"I get my own room. And it's got to be on the opposite side of the house from yours. I don't want to be able to hear you two going at it."

"Maybe a duplex would be better. I don't know if I could handle seeing your ugly mug 24/7. Or separate houses. On opposite sides of the street."

"Then you'd have to teach Charlotte, early, how to cross the street to see her favorite uncle." Riley lifted the fussing baby to his shoulder, rubbing her back.

"Look at you. The 'dad' gene hasn't skipped you after all."

"Bite me."

"Yeah, separate houses would be a must."

"You know you want me for my mad chili-cooking skills."

"I can buy a cookbook, teach myself."

"Not the same, pal. Not the same. Face it. You need me."

Sam lifted Charlotte from Riley's shoulder. Her demanding whimpers for her next meal were escalating. He bundled her into a blanket, grabbed the diaper bag he'd come over with and prepared to leave. Dropping a hand on his friend's shoulder, he squeezed.

"She needs us both. I guess it's my job to make her see that. Poor Charlotte. Craziest damned put-together family I've ever seen."

"I love you too, man. Now get the hell out of my house." Riley's voice was just a tad gruffer than usual.

• • •

Coming home to such a cozy scene, was it any wonder that Sam had the overwhelming urge to cross the kitchen and give Wynter a kiss? She wore her ratty bathrobe, her crazy hair freshly washed and already sticking up at all angles as it dried. Her skin glowed and he longed to wrap her in his arms so he could lean in close and let the scent of her bath soap tease his nostrils.

Charlotte chose that moment to let out a lusty screech, alerting her mom to the fact that they'd just slipped in the back door. Now he had an excuse to approach, not the one he would have chosen, but an excuse nonetheless. Wynter lifted her daughter from his shoulder and Sam felt a moment's jealousy as she nuzzled the infant close. Oh, to be nuzzled by the woman who was fast occupying nearly every one of his waking thoughts.

"She told me she was done visiting Uncle Riley and would like some lunch—pronto."

"Oh, she told you that, huh? That's my smart little girl."

Wynter headed for the living room and Sam trailed behind. He had some work to do but he could put it off for a bit. He waited until Wynter settled into the corner of the couch and then handed her the baby Boppy so she could nurse. It said a lot about their relationship, the routine they had developed, that she thought nothing of parting her robe to feed her child while he was still in the room. It said a lot more about him that he didn't lower himself to stare.

"How's Riley? I should have gone with you two to visit."

"He's fine and no you shouldn't have. We gave you some well-deserved down time. You should now feel unbelievably relaxed. You're welcome."

Wynter chuckled, amusement creasing the corners of her eyes. Charlotte suckled greedily, the sound bringing a fresh round of laughter. Sam watched mother and daughter, the bond mesmerizing. Wynter stroked the petal soft skin of Charlotte's cheek, working her finger into the infant's grasp. Sam sat on his end of the couch, feeling as though he were intruding. They didn't need him here, but heaven help him, he couldn't make himself get up and leave.

"I'm writing your grandmother another letter." Dread twisted its way through Sam's veins, heavy and ice cold.

"You and Charlotte are welcome to stay as long as you like. I think we've got a good thing here. We make a good parenting team." *God, was he wheedling?* The thought disgusted him.

"I agree, Sam. It's just … " She paused, seeming unsure how to proceed.

"You don't like Braeden. I get that. It's too quiet, not enough like Scallop Shores." He was starting to panic. She was going to make him babble.

"You knew my plans all along. This is nothing new." Wynter fixed him with a determined stare, held his unwilling gaze. "Come with us, Sam."

"We've talked about this. I can't go back there."

"No, actually we haven't really talked about this. We've never talked about that night. We've never talked about how you took off, how you cut ties with your grandmother, with Holt and me. It's time we talk about it, Sam."

"Now?" The word came out a squawk.

"Is there ever going to be an ideal time?" She quirked an eyebrow.

No. Because they didn't need to discuss this. Not now, not ever. Sam's focus flew to the doorway, mentally mapping an escape route. Wynter was in the middle of breastfeeding. She couldn't get up easily and chase after him. He could cite work obligations.

"I don't blame you for being scared."

"I'm not scared. What makes you think I'm scared?" Besides the fact that his voice had gone up several octaves. Geez.

"Sam, we used to be able to tell each other anything. That night we were talking about the future. We talked about how scared we were, how it was only tolerable because we were going to be facing it together."

And then he'd left her. She was kind enough not to say it out loud, but the fact was still hanging out there, shouting in his ear. *"You left your best friends. You left the girl you loved."* Okay, so she didn't know that last part, but it weighed on him, nonetheless.

"I'm sorry, Wynter. I've never apologized for what I did after that night. I am so sorry I didn't say goodbye."

"Not sorry you left. Sorry you didn't wrap it up neatly, file us away as a done deal." He could hear the disappointment in her voice, the bitterness that he had caused.

"I couldn't face you. Not after what I'd done."

"Samuel Dennis, you did *not* have anything to do with your parents' death that night."

"I know that, Wyn. I'm not saying I caused it. Or that anything I did could have prevented it."

Sam braced his elbows on his knees. Leaning down, he scrubbed at his eyes with the heels of his palms. He couldn't do this. Why was she making him? Talking about it didn't change things. His parents were still dead. Nothing would bring them back. He peered between two fingers.

She switched the baby to the other side. Waited for him to continue. Calm as could be. Like she couldn't see the turmoil he was facing. The exposed feelings, the raw nerves peeled back and bleeding. Real friends wouldn't do this to each other. Real friends would be supportive. And what? Encourage him to bury his head in the sand? Tell him it was okay to keep hiding from what happened, from what he was feeling?

He stood up from the couch, pacing to the window, to the bookcase along the side wall, and past the doorway he wished he'd escaped through before they started this conversation. He wiped sweaty palms on the back of his jeans. He worked the kinks out of his neck, wincing at the unusual loudness of the cracks and pops. He shoved a hand through hair that was way overdue for a cut.

This was why he had cut ties with his friends. Not because they were a painful reminder of his life that was, but because he knew, eventually, he'd be having this conversation. Wynter wouldn't want him to hold on to the hurt, the pain, and the guilt. The guilt he'd held on to for so long it was a part of him, impossible to separate from any other facet of his personality.

"I was supposed to die that night. Is that what you want? You want me to admit it? Okay. I cheated death."

Sam stopped treading the carpet, faced Wynter head on. The look in his eyes dared her to contradict him. Her jaw dropped. The look in her eyes was utter disbelief. *Oh, come on!* This was no big surprise.

"Is that what you think, Sam?" She shook her head vehemently. "No. There was a reason you fell asleep in my bed that night. God had other plans for you. It wasn't your time. Your life was spared."

"I was supposed to be there. If I hadn't snuck out of the house, I would have died in my sleep, the same as them. I was supposed to die that night."

In his head he was back there, that early summer day, so long ago. He'd woken up, completely disoriented. Where was he? Shit! He'd only meant to watch Wynter as she slept. He'd never meant to fall asleep beside her.

Home. He had to get home. He had to slip out of Wynter's window and down the tree, before his parents found him missing. Sam didn't want to make them angry. He'd just graduated. They were so proud. His dad told him to expect a big gift the next morning, but not to go snooping. He'd seen the look his parents had exchanged. They'd decided on this together and it was going to be huge. They were so happy. But if he disappointed them, if they found out that he'd snuck up to see Wynter, they might decide not to give it to him. He had to hurry home.

Breath coming in short pants, he turned, confused. Had to find the window.

Then suddenly Wynter was with him, wrapping her arms around him. He cupped her head in his big hand. Her hair. What had happened to her long, curly hair? She kept saying she was sorry. No. Everything would be okay if he could just get home.

"Sammy, come back to me. Please. You're scaring me."

"Have to get home. They're gonna be mad."

"They're at peace now, Sam. They are so happy. They love you. They will always love you."

He gripped her so tight he was afraid he'd leave bruises. He buried his head against her shoulder as the rest of the memories came flooding back.

It was far later than he'd realized. Dawn had turned the sky a hazy gray by the time he'd made it home. The house was so quiet. They hadn't heard him slip back inside.

That was when the alarm had gone off in his parent's bedroom. His dad had always been an early riser. Rain or shine, he ran five miles every morning. He always set his alarm for 5:30 am. Only this time, the alarm continued to blare and no one was bothering to turn it off.

Why weren't they waking up? Why were they letting the alarm clock just clamber away like a screeching banshee? Unsettled, Sam slunk down the hallway toward the last room on the end. They were sleeping so peacefully, too peacefully.

He could still see their faces, in sweet repose. If he reached out, shook their shoulders. He just had to wake them up. If only they'd wake up.

"Sam, I'm so sorry."

Wynter's voice. It grounded him in reality. It brought him back, made him realize that it was too late to save his parents. The past was in the past.

He lifted his head from her shoulder, mortified to discover that her bathrobe was soaked in his tears. He slapped at his wet eyes, turning away so Wynter wouldn't see a grown man cry. He flinched at the touch of her hand on his back. He didn't want her to see him like this. He needed to be alone.

"Yeah, so it was great reminiscing and all, but I've got to get some work done."

He swept past her on his way out of the room. Her lips were pressed tightly together, like it was taking all the strength she had not to try to continue this horribly painful conversation. Tears rolled down her cheeks.

No. He couldn't deal with this right now. Lock it away, down deep where it can't hurt. That's what you did with memories like this. He practically ran for his office, locking the door before sliding down it to crumple on the floor, where he wept for the boy who had lost both his parents to such a stupid, senseless tragedy.

Chapter 14

Sam was avoiding her. Wynter lifted a hand to knock on the closed office door and let it fall back to her side. She didn't blame him. She'd pushed him to reveal feelings that she guessed he didn't realize he had. She wasn't sorry. He couldn't avoid talking about that night forever. But he deserved a chance to retreat, time to think about his revelations.

The last of the snow was now a muddy wasteland. The white stuff had lost its charm long ago, anyway. It was time to get out of the house, explore Sam's town and actively look for signs of spring to help raise her spirits.

She'd finished her letter to Sam's grandmother and slipped in a recent photo of Charlotte for good measure. Ruby Dennis had long been on a one-person crusade to make sure that letter writing did not go the way of the dinosaurs. Emails and phone calls would have been more convenient, but Wynter treasured their correspondence and enjoyed partaking in the old-fashioned tradition.

Dropping the letter in the mailbox would have been easier, but running it all the way to the post office meant the chance to borrow Sam's car and take a little field trip into town, such as it was. Wynter bundled the baby in her car seat and headed for the barn that had been converted to a garage. She winced with each squelch of her sneakers, slowly getting covered in slime.

Backing out of the driveway, she hoped she could remember her way to town. Was it a straightaway? Didn't she have to take a left at the signpost? She sort of recalled how to get to the hospital, but that was a couple of towns over. And there was lots of farmland in between. She shrugged, sparing a quick glance at the gas gauge and geared up for an adventure.

Four houses. She'd counted. That was exactly how many residences Wynter spied on the way to town. And she'd managed to find her way, avoiding the turnoffs to the myriad farm lanes that meandered through fields of cows. Seriously, she wondered if the cow population exceeded the humans in the state of Vermont. She'd have to look that one up.

To say the town was a disappointment would be an understatement. Brick shoeboxes were arranged side by side. Every building looked exactly like the one beside it, across from it. The sleepy little town looked cold and industrial. So much potential wasted. Where they could have built window boxes to dress up the facades, there were none. Where they could have brightly colored awnings that welcomed guests, they had stark, naked doorways.

Wynter couldn't find a single bench for townsfolk to stop and rest while running their errands. Perhaps they were not encouraged to linger. Just because it was a small town did not mean it was a close town. Maybe people had no desire to stop and catch up with each other.

Pulling into the empty parking lot beside the post office, Wynter reminded herself that she was unfairly comparing Braeden to her hometown. She resolved to withhold judgment until she'd had a chance to do a little exploring. Maybe she'd find a hidden gem that made the bleak little town worth visiting.

Lucky thing she could drop her letter off in the big blue mailbox outside the door, because the post office did not open until 10am. Wynter pondered whether lugging around a heavy car seat, only to browse if no one was open yet, was worth it. She peered at the windows, trying to make out the lettering on the nondescript signage across the street.

An old plastic Coors logo was lit up in the window of a building on the corner. Hopefully it was a restaurant and not a bar. Looking both ways before crossing the street, Wynter scoffed at the wasted effort. There wasn't a car in sight, save for Sam's SUV.

Yes. Red Formica tables and sticky vinyl booths. No bar stools. Not sure where these patrons were hiding their vehicles, Wynter was surprised to find the place half full. There was no bell over the door to announce her arrival, yet every pair of eyes turned to watch her shuffle uncomfortably to the hostess station.

"You want a table?" An older, tired looking waitress appeared at her elbow, holding a menu in one hand and a carafe of coffee in the other.

A table, a booth, anything to get her out of the spotlight. "Yes, please."

The waitress walked her to a table in the back. Wynter tried smiling at the first few staring faces, but gave up when they only scowled back. Tough crowd. She set the car seat on the floor, taking a moment to tuck the fuzzy pink blanket beneath Charlotte's chin. The waitress' eyes lingered on the baby, her lips puckering in what could have been an attempt at a genuine smile but then she huffed and broke her gaze.

"Coffee?"

"I'd love some, thank you."

She shouldn't be here, on Sam's dime, as it were. She'd eaten breakfast at home so this was just wasteful. Only she needed an excuse to explore the town. Flipping open the menu, Wynter searched out the side items. Surely Sam wouldn't begrudge her an English muffin and a cup of coffee? Of course he wouldn't. Any guilt was solely on her.

"Just passing through town?" The older woman set a chipped coffee mug down in front of her with a nod in the direction of the sugar dispenser and the little bowl of non-dairy creamers.

"Staying with a friend, actually. We've been here a few months now. Well, I have." She gave the baby carrier a little bounce with her toe. "This little one only arrived about six weeks ago."

"Never seen ya before."

"Well, with Sam living out on Rockford Road, we kept getting snowed in. Not really sightseeing weather."

"Sam?" The waitress frowned.

"Sam Dennis. He's lived here for about eight years now, I guess."

"Nah. Never heard of him."

"How about Riley Tucker? They live across the street from each other."

"Nope. Him neither."

Unsure what else to say, Wynter held out the menu. She ordered an English muffin, no butter and a slice of cheese. Her waitress frowned, like she wanted to say there was a minimum order and if she wanted to eat there, she'd have to order more food.

The baby started to fuss and Wynter wished she could join her. She rocked the car seat back and forth. Why would Sam punish himself like this? Hide in a town where no one seemed to know, or care, that he even existed. This was awful.

In Scallop Shores, he'd been loved by all. He'd been on the basketball team and the baseball team, rubbing elbows with the jocks. Proud geek, he had been the one to start a chess club in high school and won trophies for math club. His family hailed back so far, Wynter wouldn't be surprised if they were some of the town's founding fathers.

Mr. Dennis had been the town vet, practicing out of an old house in town that had been in his family for generations. Sam's mom had been the police dispatcher, the voice everyone heard over their scanners whenever the police were summoned, which in their town was rarely for anything exciting. It was with bitter irony that Wynter realized the most action Scallop Shores had seen, while she'd been living there, was the call that the Dennises had asphyxiated in their sleep.

That was Sam's last memory of his hometown. Hers, as well, practically. But while it was enough to keep him away for the rest of his life, it did nothing to curb her homesickness. She still wanted to go back, now more than ever. But how to get Sam away from this awful place he chose to serve his penance? She really hoped she heard back from Ruby soon. If anyone could help her convince Sam to move back home, it was his grandmother.

•••

If he didn't stop and take a break, his eyes were going to permanently cross. Sam pushed off against the edge of the desk, sending his chair flying back a few feet. Because it was fun, he did it again. Remembering the reason he'd barricaded himself in his office sobered his mood.

Sure he'd been avoiding her but Wynter, being Wynter, was supposed to come in and get in his face. It was what she did. It was their routine. He tried to hide from the things that made him uncomfortable and she forced him to deal with it. So where was she?

The house was quiet. He hadn't heard Charlotte crying in a while. It was hardly likely that they were just napping together. They must be out. And she hadn't told him she was leaving. Good grief! They weren't an old married couple. How many times had he said exactly that to Riley? So why was he working himself into a snit now at the possibility she'd gone out without him?

Get used to it, Sammy boy. This is what it was like before she got here. This is what it's going to be like when she moves back to Scallop Shores. Leaning his head back against the leather chair, Sam pinched the bridge of his nose. His computer went into sleep mode and a photo of Wynter and the baby popped up on his screensaver.

She thought he'd told her everything about that night. She thought she understood his guilt. She had no clue he had really been in her room to finally admit his feelings for her. And there was no reason to tell her now. So why did he feel sneaky, as though he was hiding something from her?

A form of self-flagellation, Sam's mind went into the old 'what if' scenario. What if he'd had the nerve to tell Wynter he loved her that night? Would she have returned his feelings? Would he have been so anxious to run, to escape Scallop Shores and everyone that reminded him of his parents and the fact that he'd cheated death? Would she have made more of an effort to find him when he first left, not twelve years after the fact? And the kicker, would Wynter have chosen Sam over Holt? Married him? Had *his* baby?

It shouldn't even matter at this point. Sam growled, banging a fist on the armrest. He was hanging on to the past and it had to stop. Scrubbing his hands over his stubbled face, he shook his head. He needed a shower—and a toothbrush. It was time to let go of the 'what ifs' and start focusing on the 'what could bes.'

After he'd showered, shaved, and sucked down a scalding cup of coffee, Sam went in search of his girls. Yeah, they were his now and it was time to figure out a way to keep Wynter in his life.

His SUV was still in the barn so they couldn't have gone far. He'd seen the stroller, still folded, and leaning against the wall by the back door. It appeared that Riley had a couple of guests. Well, his buddy was about to get one more.

"Lucy, I'm home!" Sam let himself into Riley's kitchen.

"Go away, I have a date." Riley's voice came from somewhere in the front of the house.

Sam listened for Wynter's responding laugh, a comment, anything. Where was she? He stalked down the hall, finding his friend in the living room, a biography on Abraham Lincoln open in his lap, and Charlotte nestled in the crook of his arm.

"Where's Wyn?"

"You thought she was who I was talking about when I said date, huh?" Riley's wolfish grin grew huge. "You were jealous." His laughter grated on Sam's nerves.

"Shut up. Where is she?"

"Finally taking back what is yours, huh? Good for you, man." Riley nodded his head toward the hallway. "She went down in the basement. Said she has a surprise for me. Lots of racket. I have no idea." Riley shook his head.

As if on cue, a table saw whined loud enough to reach their ears. *What the hell?* Sam scrunched his nose and sent Riley a confused look. The other man shrugged his shoulders.

"I told you. Big racket. Been at it all morning. Tell her she better plan on cleaning up after herself. It's not like I have a way of getting down to that basement any time in the near future."

"I'll see what's going on. You good here?"

"Yeah. My date lets me do all the talking. I think this one's a keeper." Riley kissed the top of Charlotte's downy head. "Go get her, Romeo."

Sam strode for the stairs to the basement, his heart racing with worry that Wynter was taking on something far too dangerous for her to handle.

The buzzing of the saw cut off before he reached the bottom of the stairs. He steeled himself for a fight with the most stubborn woman he'd ever met. Rounding the corner, he opened his mouth to tell her exactly how crazy he thought she was to be messing with power tools, and let it hang. There might have been drool involved.

"Hey, I see you're out of your cave. No telling Riley what I'm up to, you hear?"

Nope. He wouldn't say a word. Mostly because all his blood had rushed to regions south. He'd lost all feeling in the upper half of his body, while the lower half was uncomfortably … stiff.

She stood behind a table saw, safety glasses covering her eyes. His old blue plaid flannel, barely covering a tiny white tank top, was tied in a knot at her waist. Sam looked her up and down, licking his lips as his imagination went into overdrive. She needed a tool belt. Yes. And work boots. Oh, and cut-off jeans.

"Yoo-hoo? Earth to Sam. You in there?" She'd lifted the glasses to the top of her head and set her hands on her hips.

"You've picked up some interesting new skills since high school." Sam worked his tongue around the inside of his mouth. His words felt slurred, his head definitely fuzzy.

"Who knew, right?" She hefted a stack of boards, cut to size, to the workbench against the wall. "Turns out I can DIY like a pro. Guess all those home improvement shows I've been watching have paid off." She winked as she picked up a drill and Sam had to bite back a moan.

"So what's the project?" He managed to squeeze out the question.

"Riley's got all those books and no place to store them. I'm putting some built-in shelving on either side of the big picture window in the living room. It all has to be waist-level, so I may just wrap it around the whole room."

"He's a lucky guy." Sam's sentiment was genuine.

"Jealous?" She flipped the safety glasses into place with a grin and gave the drill a brief whir.

Sam's feet were moving before he realized his intent. He grabbed the drill from Wynter's hand and set it on the bench. Slowly, he lifted the heavy plastic from her eyes, smiling with satisfaction when he realized her hooded gaze surely matched his own. He backed her up against the workbench, their bodies fitting together like a jigsaw puzzle. *Just imagine what it would be like without clothing?*

"Nah. Not jealous. It's just the two of us down here, and Riley can't make it down the stairs."

Knowing she was about to scold him for his unkind words, Sam captured her lips before she could speak. He could smell her lavender body wash. He tasted her peppermint chewing gum, stealing it out of her mouth with a swipe of his tongue. Her throaty chuckle had him straining to get closer still.

Never breaking their kiss, he swept Wynter up in his arms. She wrapped her legs around him. Yes. Just like that. Sam didn't even have to tell her what he liked.

He broke the kiss so that he could explore more of her, taste her sweet skin. Drawing her earlobe into his mouth, he sucked harder when her breathy sigh turned into a soft mewling. Their bodies were so close but he needed to be closer still. His hand was at the snap on her jeans when he realized what he was doing.

He'd waited this long, for this amazing woman. He'd saved himself for her. He knew that now. His first sexual experience was supposed to be with Wynter. But not like this. He wouldn't take her in someone else's dank basement. This was not the memory he wanted to create for his first time.

"I want you." He rested his forehead against her shoulder, taking long shuddering breaths and willing his body to calm down.

"I want you, too." Her fingers found him through the rough fabric of his jeans and it took everything he had to reach down and curl his hand around hers.

"But not like this, Wyn. You deserve better than this."

"It's okay." His body cheered as she tried to convince him with her words, and her actions, that they should continue.

"*We* deserve better than this." He couldn't even believe his brain was still functioning at this point.

Wynter unhooked her heels from behind him, lifting his head to place a soft kiss on his mouth. She held his face between her hands as she studied him. Her cheeks were flushed and her eyes overly bright. In her expression he read frustration and a promise that they would pick up where they'd left off. But she wasn't angry.

It was on the tip of his tongue to tell her he loved her. But he didn't want to scare her. For all he knew, her interest in him was purely physical. At least this way, by keeping silent, he wouldn't have to find out. It was his heart's way of protecting itself, should his plans for the future not come to fruition.

Chapter 15

"You didn't have to come all this way with me. I would have been good, just borrowing your truck."

Wynter set the baby, in her car seat, on the floor beside her chair and sat down. Sam perused the stack of magazines on the side table, selected one and laid it in her lap, before claiming the seat beside her. This was just too … comfortable. Her head screamed that it was high time she start thinking and acting independently. She was a single mom, after all. Her heart told her to grab onto Sam and not let go.

"You're welcome." He patted her knee. *Oh, honestly!*

"Wynter Grayson?"

"If you wouldn't mind watching …? " Wynter's voice trailed off as Sam stood, lifting the baby carrier, and headed for the smiling nurse. *Alright then.*

"So, I hear you thought you were too good for our little hospital? Decided to do things all on your own?" The nurse grinned. "Usually happens around here once or twice every winter. Moms think they have enough time and then Mother Nature throws a curve ball at 'em."

"It wasn't as scary as I expected it to be," Wynter admitted.

"Ah, then you had a good man there helping you." The nurse winked at Sam, who ducked his head shyly.

She left them alone so Wynter could slip into the rough, paper gown. Sam turned his back to give her privacy, focusing instead on Charlotte, who had chosen that moment to wake up from her morning nap. After yesterday's heated interlude, Wynter was more than a little disappointed that he didn't even try to catch a peek. And now she was disgusted with herself for bothering to care.

The doctor bustled in after a brief tap at the door. She headed straight for the baby, cooing and clucking and marveling at how alert she was. With a wistful sigh and a hand on her chest, she turned to address Wynter.

"You done good, Mama. How are you feeling?"

"A little tired."

"Any more bleeding?"

Wynter blushed, blurting out, "No, that stopped a few weeks ago."

"I don't have to ask if your milk supply is doing well. Those chubby cheeks tell me she's getting plenty to eat." The woman threw a grin over her shoulder at the baby.

She had Wynter slide to the edge of the table for her exam. Sam had moved the one chair in the room to the opposite corner. This time Wynter was grateful he couldn't see. She glanced over to find him watching her, smiling. Okay, she was happy that he'd come to the appointment.

"You're healing up just fine. You've gotten past the first six weeks, so you can resume sexual activity. Would you like me to write a prescription for some birth control?"

"Oh, we're not … I don't need … " Wynter was mortified.

"I understand. Some couples have difficulty being intimate again after childbirth. Especially given your circumstances, where your husband delivered the baby."

"He's not my husband," she said, miserably.

"No one is judging."

Wynter threw a look at Sam, her eyes pleading for him to rescue her.

"She'll take the prescription, Doctor."

Damn him.

The ride home was quiet. Wynter squirmed in her seat, so many emotions vying for top billing that her head swam. Excitement over the possibility of sex with Sam had her body throbbing.

Guilt over the fact that she'd never felt this giddy with Holt was like a lead weight, dragging her down. Hope for a future with a man she was beginning to realize she couldn't live without sang in her veins. And just to balance things out evenly, dread wrapped a heavy blanket around the whole package, reminding her that in order to achieve her dream of moving back to Scallop Shores, she'd have to leave Sam behind.

"I didn't mean to make you uncomfortable, put you on the spot." He'd pulled into the driveway, shut off the car and turned to face her.

She didn't want to do this now. Sitting in the enclosed space, she felt vulnerable, nervous.

"I'm fine." The words came out on a shaky squeak. *Good Lord.*

"Look, all I meant was that it would be smart to fill the prescription." He paused, not speaking again until Wynter met his gaze. "We both know it's going to happen. Some day."

She licked her lips, her mouth like dust. She nodded.

"Yeah, some day."

Sam chuckled, the deep sound reverberating through the truck's cab. Her body quivered in response. He thought this was funny? He was making light of her sudden bout of nerves?

He must have seen the storm clouds gathering in her expression, the scowl pulling her eyebrows down. He held his hands out in front of him, shaking his head.

"Hey, don't misunderstand me. It's just that I have a much bigger reason for being terrified about all this."

"What could you have to be terrified about?" She scoffed. "You're a guy. Guys think about sex … What's the statistic?" Wynter waved her hand flippantly.

"Let's just say I have a lot of catching up to do."

"Oh. Of course. I get it. It's been a while for you." She blushed, realizing what he was getting at. "You were a hermit before I forced myself back into your life."

Sam faced the windshield, stretching his legs out as much as he could beneath the steering wheel. Wynter studied his profile, his jaw tight, like he was grinding his back teeth. His eyes were closed.

"It's okay. We don't have to do this right now. Let's just go inside—" She put her hand out to open the door and let out a little squeal when Sam reached for her knee to stop her.

"No. You need to hear this. It might ... change things. You might decide you don't want this anymore."

Her heart began to thud painfully. Where was he going with this? Was he going to tell her about some venereal disease? Did he have some kinky fetish? Was it hot in here? She felt the walls of the truck closing in on her and couldn't draw a full breath of air into her lungs.

"I don't know what you're imagining, Wyn, but it's not like that." His smile was crooked, but it was there.

"Just spit it out. You're killing me here!"

"I just wanted to warn you that I'm not the most experienced guy around." He chewed on his lower lip, his attention focused on the hand that still gripped her knee.

She lifted his hand, taking it with both of her own. She brushed a thumb over the tiny hairs across his knuckles. Turning in her seat, she waited until he met her eyes. He looked so troubled. He wanted her approval.

"Sam. It's not like I have much to compare you to. I've only ever been with Holt." She paused. "I guess I just assumed you knew that."

"Well, that's one more person than I've been with." He tried to tug his hand free and she could see him retreating inside, the shame he must have felt a living, pulsing force.

"You're a virgin." She said it very matter-of-fact. "Is that all? Gosh, Sam, I've got to tell you, with that build up, I was afraid you were going to reveal some freaky secret that I wanted no part of."

"I'm a thirty-year-old virgin. That doesn't disgust you?" Again he tried to remove his hand. She placed it on her lap, wrapping the palm around her thigh and holding it there.

"With this solitary existence you've taken up, punishing yourself by living out in the boonies, it's no wonder." She stopped, blinked. "And if it's because you were saving yourself for marriage, for the right person, well, that's commendable. There are so few men like that in the world today."

He didn't say anything, just kept looking between their hands on her thigh and her face. Then it dawned on her. *She* was the right person. He had chosen her to give his virginity to. Wow. This had suddenly become a much bigger deal. It was no longer about casual sex, it was about making love. The stakes were higher.

She realized now that they couldn't just share a bed for the brief time they had together before she moved to Scallop Shores. He might think he was ready for an encounter like that. But Sam was a different kind of man. Sam was a man with morals, and principles that were old-fashioned and … refreshing.

"I can't tell what you're thinking right now. It's freaking me out." His Adam's apple bobbed in his throat.

"I'm thinking we should take our time. Make sure we're ready for this."

He muttered an expletive under his breath, turning his head to stare out the driver's side window.

"I knew you'd be disappointed."

"Samuel Dennis, where on Earth did you get that idea? I still want you, you stubborn lug!" He refused to look at her. "But I want this to be special for you. I want to do this right. You only get one first time."

"I don't deserve you." He'd turned his head and was smiling sadly at her.

Would things have been different if Sam had stayed? If the three of them had gone on to college together? She hadn't thought of him like that, back in high school, but her need of him had gone beyond casual friendship. She felt his loss so deeply that it had affected nearly every decision she had made regarding her future. Could she have loved him back then and not realized it?

And why did her head choose this moment to bring these thoughts to the forefront? She needed some time alone to sort it all out.

An all-too-familiar trumpeting sounded from the backseat, followed by an unpleasant odor. Saved by the poo! Wynter scrambled from the cab of the truck at the same time Sam flung open his own door. As they were both embarrassed, she mostly felt relieved when he quickly disappeared from view. Not the best way to wrap up such a highly charged conversation, but it provided them both the escape they needed. She reached into the backseat and hauled out her stinky daughter.

• • •

Morals sucked. He'd waited his whole adult life to share the most intimate of moments with someone he deemed worthy of the wait. That it happened to be the same person he had pictured as an idealistic teenager still shocked him. He knew Wynter was the one for him. He knew he'd never love anyone else the way he loved her. But he did not know if she felt the same way.

Sam cracked another stick across his knee and tossed the pieces in the yard waste bin. The warmth of the bright sunshine was negated by the chill wind that blew through the back yard. In like a lion … He put his back into the labor in an effort to stay warm.

So did he say 'screw it' and share what little time they might have left memorizing every detail of their developing relationship? Would that make it worse when the time came to say goodbye? Or, and this was the option that made him feel like a jerk, did he convince her to give up her dreams of raising Charlotte in Scallop

Shores to stay with him in Braeden, or somewhere they chose together?

Sam wished like hell that he could go with her. Things were good between them, really good, and if he agreed to go back to Maine, they stood a chance of making it. But the town, those memories, he was scared it would drive him insane. Every time he drove by his old house, every time he saw an ambulance, he'd remember the dread upon hearing those sirens from the quiet safety of Wynter's bedroom. He couldn't save his parents and, God help him, he still believed he should have died with them that night.

He attacked the flowerbeds with a vengeance, raking the dead leaves away from the daffodils more roughly than was necessary. Wynter was over at Riley's, working on the built-ins that she was going to surprise him with. Wynter and power tools. Sam groaned, his jeans feeling a tad too tight. Yeah, teenage Sam had much tamer fantasies about the girl next door. Teenage Sam wouldn't have known what to do with a woman like Wynter.

Quite honestly, he didn't know where all this confidence stemmed from. It wasn't like he had the experience to back it up. Thinking about Wynter, about being with her, it just felt right. They were meant to be.

Then why did she marry Holt? The niggling doubt sent unwelcome chills down his neck. Back then, he'd been just as close to Holt as he was to Wynter. Was he betraying his friend by stealing the woman he'd loved? Could he get away with telling himself Holt would want him to take care of his wife and daughter?

Guilt. If anyone was intimately familiar with this cruelest of emotions, it was Sam. Survivor's guilt. Guilt over leaving Wynter and Holt. Guilt from avoiding his sister, his nephews, and his grandmother. The different facets of guilt that made up his life were getting too numerous to mention. It was both physically and mentally exhausting. Sam knew he should just let it go. And he wanted to. For Wynter.

The sickeningly sweet crooning of some boy band from years past had Sam dropping the rake and scrambling in his pocket to answer his phone. Wynter's idea of a joke. She saw Sam leaving his cell phone out as an invitation to mess with his ring tone—the more obnoxious the better. This was worse than the Village People song she'd stuck him with last week. He hit the answer button without even checking the screen.

"What crap is this? A boy band? I could have hurled all over my phone, thank you very much."

"Samuel?" His grandmother's voice sounded confused, a little annoyed.

Whoops.

"Hey, Grandma. Sorry about that. I thought you were Wynter."

"Not even in my prime." He could hear the laughter in her tone, could picture her shaking her head in mirth.

"I'm sorry I haven't called in a while." Might as well get the apology out there before she could ask for it.

"That's all right, actually. I understand you've been quite busy."

Paulie had been filling their grandmother in on his private life again. Leave it to his sister to butt in and stir things up.

"I received a letter from Wynter."

Sam stumbled, casting his gaze around for somewhere to sit before he fell. Is this what a panic attack felt like? His lungs were on fire and whatever breath he could draw was raspy and weak. It was as though a thousand ants were crawling over his skin, behind his ears, across his scalp. His knees felt liquid and he let himself sink to the ground with a grunt.

"Samuel?"

"Still here, Grandma. She wants to run your bookstore. I know."

"Well, then you can tell her it's hers. I've waited until I was sure she was ready. She's a bright girl. Good head on her shoulders. And now she's a single parent who could definitely use a break. Unless … ?" She let the question dangle.

"Yeah, she wants it. She'll do a great job. You're the best, Grandma. We owe you big."

She said nothing. The silence was even more unnerving than her grand news.

"I was hoping … Well, it's none of my business. An old woman's foolish dream."

"I can't do it, Grandma. I can't go back there." He put his elbows on his knees, hanging his head.

"I was going to say that I hoped you and Wynter would find that spark you once had. I would have laid odds that you were the one she was crazy about, not that other boy, Holt."

It was on the tip of his tongue to call his grandmother crazy, but he bit it back in time.

"Things between us aren't like that, Grandma." As much as he wanted them to be.

"So you're just going to let her go?" It grated on Sam that she sounded as though she were speaking to a young child.

"It's what she wants, Grandma. I want her to be happy."

"Could *you* make her happy?"

Could he? He'd like to think so.

"It doesn't matter, anymore. Her heart is already in Scallop Shores."

"And what about once she's here, will your heart be in Scallop Shores, as well?"

That wasn't fair.

"Samuel, you had no control over losing your parents. It was tragic, but it wasn't your fault. If you let Wynter go without telling her how you feel, without even trying to get past whatever this is that keeps you from home, well, that's on you, Sammie."

She was right. It hurt to admit it, but she spoke the truth.

"Pass on my message for me, won't you? The job is hers if she wants it."

"I will, Grandma."

"I miss you, Samuel." She sounded so old, tired.

"I love you, Grandma." Tears stung the backs of his eyelids as regret washed over him. He hadn't seen his grandmother in so very long. God, how he missed her!

Sam turned off the phone, holding it in his palm as he stared moodily at the skinny stem of a struggling new daffodil.

"Who ya talking to?" Wynter had snuck up on him from the driveway.

"My boss. New project in the works. We should celebrate."

"You didn't seem exactly happy about it." She frowned.

"You know how it is, big bucks coming in but long hours to earn them. Just trying to wrap my mind around it." His smile fell flat.

He'd just lied to his best friend. And to make matters worse, he had no intention of telling her that the bookstore was hers. His grandmother had wanted him to take control of the situation, to ensure himself a favorable outcome. He had no doubt she'd flay his hide for manipulating things this way, but he was buying himself some time. He needed to make Wynter fall in love with him. Then maybe she'd give up the idea of going back to Scallop Shores. She'd understand the subterfuge in time, right?

Chapter 16

She smelled like baby puke. Wynter leaned her head against the door to the nursery, breathing a sigh of relief that Charlotte had finally drifted off. She just wanted to jump in the shower, get into her pajamas and talk Sam into a cuddle on the couch. Maybe with a little kissing. Or a lot of kissing.

Good grief. She was bone tired and embarrassingly smelly. Sex should have been the last thing on her mind. But just thinking about Sam had her willing to trade that most valuable of commodities, sleep, for a little alone time with her man. Her man.

She'd never craved Holt's touch the way she did Sam's. Sex with Holt had been pleasant. Wynter cringed. What kind of description was that? The guy knew his way around a woman's body. But her reaction had been purely physical.

She understood why now. She had loved Holt. But she'd never been *in love* with him. Sharing her body with him had been a duty, a wife's responsibility. Sam wasn't even her husband, but a connection was there that had never existed between her and Holt. As was the case of late, thoughts of Sam had her tingling, squirming.

"Hey, Wyn, can you come in here?"

See? Just his voice could curl her toes. Wynter smiled, turning toward the bedroom at the end of the hall. She'd just peek in, tell him she was in desperate need of a shower. A strange glow lit Sam's room from within. Shuffling forward, her heart raced with equal parts fear and excitement. What was he up to?

Candles. The room was filled with them. And the bathroom too, by the looks of it. Wynter sniffed the air. Cinnamon? And some kind of pine? Every surface was covered with tiny tea lights, votives in holders and regular water glasses, and jars from her favorite candle company of all time.

"They're Christmas scents, I know. It's all I had. Paulie sent me a buttload so I'd be prepared in the event of a blizzard." Sam dug a toe into the carpet and looked up sheepishly. "It's too much. I can put them out."

"No! Please leave them. I love them. I love Christmas scents, flavors, everything about Christmas." She stepped into the room, turning in a slow circle. If it was possible for a smile to spread from her face to the rest of her body, then it did. She felt the smile in her heart and it warmed her and filled her with a sense of belonging, of purpose.

"I ran a bubble bath for you. Take your time." Sam held up the baby monitor he'd swiped from her bedroom.

"Sam, are you … Is this … " Afraid to look him in the eye, she twisted her fingers together into knots. Her eyes darted from one flickering flame to the next.

He tossed the monitor on the mattress and strode toward her, taking her hand in one of his. Reluctantly, she met his gaze. His grin was fortifying. Reaching up with his thumb, he worked her bottom lip out from between her teeth, rubbing it slowly. Wynter held her breath.

"Take your bath, Wyn. I'll be waiting." The kiss he dropped on her lips was full of promise.

The sudden rush of heat between her legs made her knees wobbly. She nodded, concentrating on putting one foot in front of the other as she made her way into the steamy bathroom. Was she supposed to shut the door? Would that be rude?

She glanced back to find Sam standing in the center of the bedroom, his hooded eyes watching her every move. Emboldened by his gaze, she left the door open and peeled off her clothes, one item at a time. Automatically, her hand reached out to cover her tummy pooch. Sam's tongue darted out to wet his lips. Had he gotten closer to the doorway? Wynter's stomach lurched and nerve endings all along her skin stood at attention. And this was how he affected her with just a look?

Careful not to slip, Wynter slid a foot into the foamy water. This time, in addition to the pine and cinnamon wafting through the thick air, she picked out vanilla and … was that bayberry? It should have been a chaotic, overwhelming mix of scents, but somehow it actually fit. Her body sank into the bubbles. She let her head fall back, the hot water tickling her chin. Her eyelids drifted shut.

Her ears were beneath the water, but she knew the moment Sam entered the bathroom. Suddenly shy, she wasn't sure if he intended to join her in the massive soaking tub or just sit and watch her bathe. Her eyes remained closed as she waited for him to make the first move.

"You're so beautiful."

Good first move.

Wynter cracked an eye open and peered up at Sam, who was on his knees, his elbows resting on the edge of the tub. She glanced down to see if any of her lady parts were sticking out of the bubbles, thinking that was what he was referring to. Nope. Actually, his eyes had never left her face.

"I was wondering … " His voice trailed off. Spots of color bloomed on his cheeks. "I wanted to try something."

She sucked in her breath, rising out of the water a bit, panic awakening a flight or fight response within her. *Was this a kinky something?* Just as quickly she shook that thought from her head. All of this was new to Sam. Of course he was nervous.

"Would you let me wash your hair?"

Wait, what? Okay, she hadn't been expecting that. She blinked him back into focus, as a broad smile slowly spread across her face. Why, yes, yes he could wash her hair. What a delicious idea. Her heart tripping in her chest, she nodded.

Wynter slid lower in the water until her hair was floating around her. For the first time in forever she wished it were longer again, able to swirl through the water, the strands long, silky, and incredibly sexy. Her spiky cut now felt boyish, butch. She sat up, drawing her knees to her chin and hugging them against her body.

"I remember your hair when we were in high school. You always kept it down with that big, fat headband to keep it all in place."

He liked it better longer too. A frown pulled at the edges of her mouth.

"Heck, you could have just tumbled out of bed and never brushed it. It was always the color that got to me."

She chanced a look through her lashes. Sam's eyes were bright but his smile had that faraway look that told her he was more in the past than in the moment. He reached for the shampoo in the corner and drizzled a little directly on top of her head. Wynter couldn't help the giggle that burst out. It tickled. Who knew she had such a sensitive scalp? Shivering, she concentrated on getting her head back in the moment.

"Fire and … life. That's what I always thought of when I thought about the color of your hair. You always looked so full of life."

"Did you think of my hair often, Sam?" She'd meant it as a joke but the way his fingers hesitated, Wynter knew she'd struck a chord.

"Well, when you have hair the color of molten lava, it tends to be a focal point." He quirked one side of his mouth up, a funny half-smile.

And then his fingers began to tunnel through, massaging her scalp and she could no longer focus on anything but pure sensation. She purred—she was sure of it. And she didn't care. Sam was working magic and she hoped he'd never stop. His blunt fingernails raised goose bumps over every surface of her skin as he scratched them over the top of her head, multiple circles swirling in tandem. It was luxurious. The purr turned into a deep-throated moan. Wynter's tongue slipped out to wet her suddenly parched lips.

Sam's fingers pressed harder. Another quick glance told her this one-sided foreplay must have been torture on him. His eyes were nearly black with need. His nostrils flared and the delicious way he nibbled at his lip had her wondering what it would feel like were he to nibble at her the same way. Yes, it was time to wrap up this bath.

"I think I should wait for you … in the other room." His voice had come out strangled. He seemed to be struggling for every breath he took.

"I'll be quick."

Sam gave a hard nod, fixed his gaze on her mouth, and then, as if he were fighting a losing battle, cupped her soapy head and drew her in for a soul-searing kiss. Just as quickly he let her go, both of them shaking. With a last searching look he turned and hurried from the room. Wynter could see him just beyond the doorway. He was pacing.

She ducked under the water, rinsing the shampoo from her hair, every touch a torturous reminder of how it felt to be under Sam's talented ministrations. She thrashed her head from side to side, in a terrible hurry to finish, to get back to him.

Screw conditioner. She couldn't take the time. She slapped a handful of soap on her skin and slicked it across her body, using the slippery solution to get the job done as fast as possible. Her every thought, every need, was focused on that man in the next room and how badly she wanted to be with him. She'd stepped into the bathtub with every intention of worrying through what was about to happen. But Sam had made her forget all of that.

Slipping her arms into the old flannel robe that smelled just like him, she belted the sash, hugged her belly and willed the butterflies to settle down. She felt like she'd been waiting for this one moment all her life. Emerging from a cloud of steam, spying Sam waiting for her by the edge of the bed, Wynter realized that, yes, she had been waiting just for this exact moment. She had to fight the urge to run across the carpet to him.

• • •

She exited the bathroom on a cloud of steam, the sweet smell of vanilla announcing her arrival. Turning to face her, Sam had to stifle a groan. Wynter was wearing his bathrobe. He'd never be able to wear it again without thinking of this moment, and how hot she looked in it. At this rate he was going to drool. He was going to embarrass himself and slurp all over her like a dog.

Get it together, man! It's Wynter. Which was exactly why his hormones were in overdrive and his nerves were frayed. Here was the woman he had dreamt of his whole life, the woman he had thought out of reach, an impossibility. Now she was in his bedroom, in his robe, wearing nothing beneath but a sultry smile.

Suddenly the holiday candles couldn't have been more appropriate. It was Christmas. It was his birthday. It was every holiday and special anniversary wrapped into one incredible evening. Sam took it all in, memorizing the pools of light, the mix of scents, the feel of the carpet beneath his feet, the rosy hue of Wynter's glowing skin. He wanted to remember this night forever.

Her footsteps faltered as she drew closer. Sam opened his arms, sighing as her body melted into his. His fingertips grazed over the slightly nubby fabric of his older-than-dirt robe. He had to fight the urge to tear the rag right off her. The only sound in the room was his own labored breathing. He slowed his movements, resting his chin on top of Wynter's head as he took a moment to refocus. *Dial it back, man. You're going to scare the crap out of her.*

"Are you … Is this okay?" Her voice was barely audible, her hands sweeping across his shoulders and down his back in what he realized was meant to be a soothing gesture.

She thought *he* was scared. He'd never been more ready in his life. Sam would have laughed if he didn't think it would completely kill the mood.

"This is so very much okay." And he could tell the moment she saw the absolute sincerity in his eyes.

Enough talking. Sam bit back a growl as he swept Wynter up against him, her toes scrabbling for purchase against the tops of his feet. He cut off her squeal with a searing kiss, his temperature rising when she hooked one leg behind him as though she were going to crawl up his body.

Walking forward, he reached the bed, tumbling them both to the mattress. Wynter's fingers crawled beneath his sweatshirt, tickling and teasing at the same time. He released her long enough to yank the fleece over his head. She pounced on his bare skin, as though she couldn't get enough of the feel of it. Sam knew the grin on his face was ridiculously cheesy.

He should be nervous. He should be worried about whether he was doing anything wrong. He'd waited his whole life for this moment. Surely there were ten million ways he could screw it up. But one look at Wynter, her eyes shining with excitement, her hands unable to keep still, Sam knew he had nothing to fear.

Kissing a trail down her neck, he parted the robe, pushing the fabric off one creamy shoulder. She shivered. Uncovering more skin, Sam traveled lower, kissing here, darting his tongue out there. He was about to draw one rosy nipple into his mouth when he felt Wynter tense, her small hands suddenly pushing against his shoulders. What was the matter?

She looked down at him, her head twitching in a slight back and forth motion, embarrassment etched into her features. It took Sam's passion-filled brain a moment to process this response. And then he too was embarrassed. He tried to look away but Wynter cupped his head in her hands and pulled him back up, until they were face to face again. She laid a kiss on him that brought him right back to that spot where he couldn't remember his own name.

Within moments they were entwined, skin on skin. The contrast, his rough and coarse, to her silken and soft, was mind blowing. Sam could go on touching this gorgeous woman forever. But when her bold hand reached down to stroke him, he knew there were more intimate treasures to explore. She rolled to her back, invitation clearly written into the gesture, as her questing fingers never let go of their prize.

This was it. Just seconds before, Sam's lungs were working like bellows, his breath coming hard and fast. Now, as he looked down at the woman he knew he never wanted to live without, stars danced in front of his eyes from lack of oxygen.

"Breathe, baby," she coaxed.

And he did. His brief moment of overwhelming fear dissipated as quickly as it had come on. Bracing on his arms, Sam rose above Wynter. Their eyes locked. He poured his feelings into that one look, his love, his trust, his vulnerability. He gave her everything.

"I love you, Sam."

On those words he joined with her, experiencing the headiest rush he'd ever felt in his life. This was what he'd been waiting for. And it was more than worth the wait. This was where he belonged, where he was meant to be. Cushioned in warmth, surrounded by the intoxicating aroma of vanilla and Wynter, encouraged by the symphony of her cooing, moans, and soft sighs, Sam felt himself racing toward a pinnacle he wasn't ready to reach. If he could freeze any moment in time, this would be the one.

This first time together came to a peak, and they were both replete, chests rising and falling in tandem as they fought to catch their breath. Wynter's head rested on his shoulder, her spiky hair tickling him under the chin. She'd thrown a leg over his and curled an arm across his body. She hummed softly in his ear, a sound of pure contentment.

Drowsy, Sam fought to stay awake. He knew men got a bad rap for not holding up their end of things, be it post-coital conversation or cuddling, and he didn't want to start out being like 'those men.' Then he realized that humming he'd recently found so adorable had turned into an even more charming snore. She'd fallen asleep before him!

So much for the requisite, 'Was it good for you?' conversation. Darned if he didn't feel just a bit disappointed. Grinning at the direction of his thoughts, Sam chuckled to himself, resolving to use the opportunity to tease Wyn just a little bit, come morning.

He knew they only had an hour or so to nap before Charlotte woke for her next feeding. Shaking off the drowsiness in order to keep his girls safe, Sam got up and blew out all the candles before climbing back into bed. He hauled Wynter across his chest and wrapped his arms around her, holding tight. As he drifted off to sleep, he thanked God for giving him a second chance with the woman of his dreams.

Chapter 17

This was it. She'd stained the built-ins a few days ago, and with Sam's help got them all upstairs. Now all that was left was to load the new shelves with Riley's vast collection of books. And hope her estimates were correct and there was enough room for everything—with room to grow. It had not escaped her notice that Riley had received five new shipments from eBay since she had started her cataloging project a few months ago.

It had been so much fun that she almost felt bad about taking her new friend's money. But she couldn't lose sight of her goals at this point. She had socked away every nickel. Yeah, the built-ins had been a freebie. Unbelievably, Riley had been sitting on the materials all along. Sam had chipped in for the wood stain. The labor had been pure love.

Wynter looked over her hard work, nodding and smiling. Now this was an addiction she could get behind. Collecting books. Wistfully, she ran a hand over the deep cherry finish, imagining a custom set of built-ins for her own house. Someday.

"When are you going to learn to read, Miss Princess?" She looked down at her daughter, strapped into her bouncy seat and kicking for all she was worth.

The kid was off to a good start that was for sure. Just last night, Wynter had walked in to find Sam seated in her rocking chair, Charlotte cradled in one arm and a dog-eared copy of *The Hobbit* in his other hand. She'd leaned against the doorframe and was soon lost somewhere in Middle Earth. Sam's voice rumbled deep when he spoke for Thorin, king of the dwarves. He pitched it higher, almost child-like, when in the role of Bilbo the hobbit. She could have listened to him read forever.

"Sam sure spoils you, doesn't he, Sweetness?" Wynter crooned.

"'Course he does. He loves her." She whirled around, a hand fluttering up to her throat.

"You shouldn't sneak up on a girl like that," she snapped. Her heart was racing to catch up with the beats it had lost when it had jumped out of her chest.

"Why not? It's fun." Riley flashed her a cheeky grin and a wink. She rolled her eyes. Heaven help the woman that ever saddled herself with this one!

The motor on his chair whirred to life as he wheeled into the room. A drawn out whistle was Riley's only comment as he inspected the empty shelving. Wynter watched him test the heights and smiled with him when he realized he'd have no problem reaching any of them.

"Marry me, Wyn." He placed a hand over his heart and batted his eyelashes.

"I beg your pardon?" She scoffed off the attention, settling herself on the floor in front of the baby.

"Unless Sam's beat me to the punch?" He let the question hang, clearly hoping for some juicy tidbit of information.

"You're incorrigible. You know that, right?"

"Only a matter of time, really. I mean the guy has loved you since the dawn of time." Riley had drawn up beside the bouncy seat, forcing Wynter to look up in order to converse with him.

"He … We're … Things are good, but … I'm afraid I don't know what you're talking about." For reasons she couldn't understand, Wynter felt a prick of guilt.

"Surely he's told you that he had a thing for you in high school, right?" She narrowed her eyes and waited for him to continue. "He was going to tell you the night his parents died. It was why he'd snuck over to see you."

She knew she should be embarrassed that Sam had discussed this with Riley, but who else did he have, really? Getting up, she paced to the window at the other end of the room. She could just make out Sam's old farmhouse across the road.

"No, he never told me that. He was nervous. I guess I just thought it had to do with college and graduating, the whole 'now we're grown ups' thing." She gripped the edge of the windowsill, staring out at the forsythia in the corner of the yard, the buds open just enough to reveal a peek of yellow.

For the hundredth time since she'd descended on Braeden, Wynter wondered what might have been. She was becoming more and more convinced that if Sam had joined them at UCLA, as planned, things between them would have developed sooner. Her marriage to Holt would never have happened. She wouldn't have settled for less than true love.

When they were growing up, Sam had always encouraged her to dream big. They'd talk for hours about what they wanted out of life. He knew her love of books and her love of her hometown, and what the perfect marriage of those two passions would be like. He knew exactly how much she wanted to run that bookstore once Ruby felt ready to retire.

Once Sam had disappeared, reaching out for her goals didn't seem quite so important. She'd lost her spark, her drive. Holt was too busy chasing his own dreams to give much thought to hers. Holt's dreams had kept them in California. It wasn't until he was gone, until Wynter was desperate to find a solution that would keep her and her precious baby off the streets, that she thought about making her dreams a reality.

Resting her forehead against the cool glass of the front window, Wynter could just make out the chirp of the robins, foraging for worms on the muddy lawn. She could hear Riley behind her, making silly noises to entertain Charlotte.

These past few weeks with Sam had reminded her that they shared a special connection. He made her want to reach for the stars. He made her want to be the best mother she could be, the best provider for her little girl. Yet this time with him also showed her how much she needed Sam in her life again, in Charlotte's life.

She swept a troubled gaze around the room. Beyond getting the books up onto the shelves, there wasn't anything more Wynter could do for Riley. The paltry sum she'd saved to move back to Scallop Shores wasn't nearly enough to get her started. Not unless she knew she had a job and a place to stay. Why hadn't she heard back from Ruby yet? The woman was a stickler for manners and would have felt obligated to answer, even if it was to let her down gently … again.

And the more time she spent here in Braeden, the more she didn't want to leave. Sam was here. Her sweet Sam. Riley too. Crusty ex-military with a gooey center. She felt closer to them than her own family. Surely it wouldn't be considered settling if she were to stay for the people she had grown to love?

Charlotte giggled, causing Wynter to whirl around and gasp. Riley had coaxed out her baby's first real laugh. Her eyes met his, the shock and wonder she saw showing her that he understood the import of the situation. Unbuckling the seat, she scooped the infant into her arms, her own laughter bubbling to the surface.

"You've reached a milestone, little one. Do you realize how amazing that is? You love your Uncle Riley, don't you, baby girl? Mommy loves him too."

Curling her daughter against her side, Wynter wrapped her other arm around Riley, kissing him loudly on his whiskered cheek. He sputtered and slapped at her arm, but she could see that he was pleased.

"Hey, what am I paying you for? Give me that little bundle of sugar and get to work putting my books away. Those shelves look downright naked."

Okay, so it wasn't Scallop Shores, but the tiny town of Braeden had Sam and Riley. Maybe it was time to give it another shot. Sam had always told her to dream big. Well, here was a crazy idea: opening a bookstore right here in blink-and-you-miss-it downtown Braeden. How was that for big, Sam?

• • •

Sam opened the sticky plastic menu, closed it, then opened it again. He still wasn't quite sure how they'd gotten here. In all the years he'd known Riley, the man had never left the safety and comfort of his own house. His friend kept a low profile, much like himself, so to see him sitting at this table, in the middle of a restaurant full of gawping strangers, really blew him away.

As a matter of fact, the prickly marine that he'd known and loved had turned into more of a teddy bear now that Wynter and Charlotte were around. He sort of missed the barking and snarling that indicated Riley was in a good mood. Before, when he was in a snit, he'd just lock Sam out.

Sure, he looked uncomfortable as hell, sitting here in full view of the scattering of townsfolk that stared as though they had never seen a man in a wheelchair before. But he was here. This was monumental. This was … eerie. Sam looked down at the table, where Wynter covered one of Riley's hands with her own. A lifeline. God, he loved her.

"Save room for dessert, gentlemen. I heard the pies are to die for." Her smile was beatific.

"Perfect. I'd like to die about now." Riley stuck a finger in between his T-shirt and his Adam's apple, pulling it away like it was choking him.

"Oh, you're doing just fine. Ignore those bad-mannered busybodies. They just don't know you yet."

"Who says I want to give them the chance?" Riley hunched down in his chair, a childish pout on his full lips.

"I'm with Ri on this, babe. You've got to admit this atmosphere is a little … creepy." Sam arched a brow, daring her to prove him wrong.

"Hey, I'm not the one who chose this town to hide out in. Creepy is as creepy does."

Her laughter trilled out. Sam shook his head, sharing a brief look with Riley before focusing his attention on the menu.

"Oh, look Riley. They have meatloaf. I wonder if it's as good as your mother used to make." At Sam's blank stare, Wynter added, "It's his favorite dinner. What he always used to ask for on his birthday."

He always thought chili was Riley's favorite dinner. When had Wynter become the expert on all things Riley Tucker? And when had Sam started treating it like a competition? The baby began to fuss in her car seat and Sam automatically reached out a toe to set it in motion.

Tuning out the nosy restaurant patrons, he took stock of his surroundings. God, when was the last time he'd eaten a meal out? Here? Never. Bubblegum-popping oldies music scratched out of the speakers. Cherry red vinyl covered nearly every surface. Their waitress glared at them from the counter, her beehive hairdo as stiff as her spine. An assortment of pies perched by the register, supported on thick, glass pedestals.

"What are you getting, Sam?"

"Hmm?" He pulled his gaze away from a larger-than-life print of Elvis.

"The menu? What are you going to order?" Wynter's mouth twitched.

They were out of their element, him and Riley both. She had to be enjoying this.

"What are we doing here, again?" He tried to keep the exasperation out of his voice. Wynter never did anything for purely selfish means. She always had their best interests at heart.

"We're celebrating." She beamed.

"Right. The successful completion of my kick-ass built in shelves by my sexy DIY-er. You have to see them now, filled with my books."

"Yeah, I know … Kick ass." Sam growled. Wynter was *his* sexy DIY-er. Jealousy flared and a gnawing need to hurt his newest friend was growing inside him.

"Down, boy!" Riley winked. "Everyone knows she's your woman. I've got no designs." He held his hands up in mock surrender.

A delicate blush rose on Wynter's pale cheeks. She rolled her eyes but it was clear she didn't mind the attention one bit.

"We're also celebrating a huge milestone in little Charlotte's life. Her first laugh, courtesy of one Riley Tucker." She squeezed Riley's hand and gave him an adoring grin.

"Yeah, if I had to laugh at anyone for the first time, it'd be at Ri. Good call, baby girl."

"And what milestone was it she gave you again? First blow out? Or was it first puke? I can never remember. Oh, wait! It was both." Riley settled back in his wheelchair, his chuckle drawing the attention of the other diners. Only this time, Sam's makeshift family chose not to care.

"I could go for a nice, greasy burger. Extra pickles. Do they do onion rings here?" He ran a finger down the list of sides, his mouth starting to water when he found the selection he was looking for.

"Mmm, a cheeseburger sounds incredible."

Uh huh. The way she purred that last sentence sounded incredible. Sam squirmed in his seat, spearing Wynter with a look that left no question as to what he was thinking. Her irises darkened and he knew she was revisiting a memory of the two of them together. He also knew they'd be making more memories later tonight.

"Third wheel, here, feeling more than a tad uncomfortable," sang out Riley.

Sure he was. His friend seemed to be taking an inordinate amount of pleasure in spoiling the moment, especially given the sly grin on his ugly mug. Sam was starting to see what it would have been like to have a brother growing up. An annoying brother.

"So I was wondering if we might take a little walk around town after dinner." Wynter's suggestion had him refocusing his attention.

Sam looked up, abruptly. The two of them? Alone? As in a date?

"Aw, just rub salt into it, why don't you?" Clearly Riley was thinking along the same lines.

Wynter blinked distractedly. She looked from Sam to Riley and back again before realization dawned and she ducked her head shyly.

"Seriously, guys? I just thought we should do a little exploring. See what the town has to offer."

"Not much," Sam grunted.

"Probably could use a good bookstore, though. Dontcha think, Sammy boy?"

Sam could have leaned across the table and kissed the man. Why the heck hadn't he thought of that? The closer Wynter had been to finishing her project for Riley, the more panicked Sam had become. How were they going to keep her in Braeden? What about this pitiful excuse for a town could entice her to stay?

"That's exactly what I was thinking, Riley." Her excitement was contagious.

Even the surly waitress couldn't douse the party atmosphere that surrounded their little table. She took their orders and refilled their drinks. Sam could tell she was memorizing as much as possible to be able to return to the kitchen with some gossip about the new folks.

Wynter had unstrapped the baby from her car seat and was bouncing her on her shoulder. Riley was trying to talk her into a military-book themed store. This led them to start trying to outdo each other with oddly themed bookstores. Just cookbooks. Only dictionaries. A tribute to Dr. Seuss.

"We don't have to stay in Braeden, you know." His suggestion was voiced quietly, once the laughter had died down.

This time, thankfully, Riley kept his mouth shut.

"Not Scallop Shores, but … Scallop Shores-ish?" Her smile was equal parts sad and hopeful. Would she go for it?

"One big happy family?" He wiped his sweaty palms against the stiff denim of his jeans.

"I'd like that." And she grabbed for one of his hands beneath the table, lifting it to the surface before doing the same with Riley.

"Aw, gushy crap. I'm gonna need another beer." Riley signaled for the waitress with his free hand, never even attempting to slip out of Wynter's grasp, Sam noticed.

Survivor's guilt had caused Sam to push his sister and his grandmother away. He'd lived in solitude for so long he'd thought he hadn't needed anyone else. Then Wynter swept back into his life, reforging relationships, building a family where he never expected to find one. And that's what they were. One big happy family. For the first time since his parents' death he longed to reach out to Paulie and his grandmother. He didn't want to be alone anymore.

Chapter 18

Wynter settled into the fancy ergonomic chair in Sam's office. He'd offered her the use of his computer to do a little research. It had been a few days since she'd dragged the menfolk out to dinner, and she was anxious to put some ideas to the test.

Her original assessment of the bleak stretch of businesses that made up downtown Braeden was seconded by Sam and Riley. The entire vibe was depressing and downright hostile. They had agreed this was not the town to raise Charlotte. Collectively, as the makeshift family they had become.

Wynter recalled, with a smile, how Sam pointed out the lack of color in the buildings, the absence of flowers or any kind of decoration to spruce up the local businesses. He regaled Riley with tales of Scallop Shores, the friendly rivalry of the shop owners as they tried to out-beautify their neighbors. The brilliant colors of the awnings. The whiskey barrels full of riotous blooms. The intricately carved signs, overhead.

Riley had cast a look around, his frown showing just how unimpressed he was with Braeden. He grudgingly admitted it was a little early for fresh flowers but insisted there were other ways to make a building stand out. He'd asked her what she would do if she owned a business on this monochromatic street.

Wrapping her fingers around a cup of hot coffee, Wynter leaned down and let the rising steam tickle her nose. Charlotte seemed to be doing just fine with a little caffeine mixed into her breast milk, God bless her! And so she breathed in the comforting scent of roasted beans, the flavored creamer adding a hint of nut to the mix. Yet another thing Braeden was missing—a decent coffee shop.

She thought of Ruby's bookstore. The Book Nook was painted on the huge storefront window, gold lettering and gorgeous script. A brilliant, emerald green awning stood out against the lighter colors on either side. Ruby always spent a great deal of time designing the front window. Spine-tingling horror novels matched with an equally chilling Halloween display, for example. One year she even set up a bed in the window to recreate a scene from "Twas The Night Before Christmas." Visions of sugarplums, indeed!

Wynter had a notebook full of her own ideas. She'd always imagined it would be The Book Nook where her ideas would take root. It was odd, and more than a little scary to be thinking of setting up shop elsewhere. But if it meant keeping her new family together, then that's what she'd have to do. She refused to acknowledge the niggling voice in her head that chided her for settling for less than her dreams.

No. She wasn't settling. Scallop Shores had given her a wealth of happy memories and the foundation for the kind of childhood she knew she wanted Charlotte to have. Surely there had to be small towns scattered throughout New England that were comparable to her hometown. Wynter just wished it didn't feel quite so much like she was cheating on Scallop Shores by considering life in a new town.

She wasn't even sure where to start looking. Census logs? Maps of the states, showing each town by population? Scrunching up her nose and tucking a strand of hair behind her ear, she brought up the search engine screen and frowned at the blinking cursor. Head back to Maine? Would Sam be open to even living in the same state he'd worked so hard to leave behind?

It would be nice to live on the coast again. If Wynter closed her eyes, she could almost hear the crash of the waves against the rocks during a storm. The sweet perfume of the beach roses, the sugary scent of pulled taffy from the penny candy store. She could even remember the differences in the feel of the sand beneath her feet, depending on which stretch of beach she was traversing. Harbor Beach had the coarsest sand, Long Beach the hardest packed, and Short Beach had the softest sand to walk on. Though with all the shops and attractions along Short Beach, it was hard to find time to sit and relax by the water.

Wynter took a sip of coffee, gagging over how cold it had gotten. She'd spent more time traipsing down memory lane than she'd realized. The baby would be wanting to eat soon and she'd made no headway in her search for a new hometown. Maybe she should save this until Sam could join her, after they put Charlotte to bed for the night. Then again, she could think of better ways to spend their precious one-on-one time.

Her cheeks were flushed and she knew the smile on her face was a goofy one. Her thoughts already headed down an equally unproductive track, Wynter nearly fell out of her chair when Sam's cell phone rang. He'd left it behind again. She'd never known anyone who misplaced their phone so often. It made messing with his ringtone way too easy.

Caller ID showed it was Sam's sister, Paulie. Glancing toward the doorway, not picking up the sound of footsteps that would suggest Sam was trying to reach his phone in time, Wynter shrugged and hit the answer button.

"Hey, Paulie. It's Wyn. I'm not sure where Sam has gotten off to."

"Wynter, how are you? How is that delicious little girl of yours? I just want to eat her up, every time Sam sends me a new picture."

Unaware that he'd been sending photos of Charlotte to his family, Wynter had to swallow hard past the lump in her throat. He must really think of her baby as his, too. Oh yeah. She was totally smitten.

"Charlotte is absolutely wonderful. I swear she's gaining a pound a day. She's such a good eater and she's already sleeping for blessedly long stretches. We just love her."

"I'm so happy for you. For all of you." Paulie's voice held a hint of confusion.

"What is it, Paulie? Everything is great here. Are you worried about Sam?"

"No. Sam sounds thrilled that you're back in his life. It's the happiest I've heard him in years. It does my heart good. It's just that I'm wondering what your plans are."

"Plans? As in the future? Funny you should mention that. We were just talking about finding a new town to live in, a place just like Scallop Shores." Wynter hoped it wouldn't sting too much for Paulie to hear that Sam wanted to move … Just not near his family.

"But what about The Book Nook? I thought you wanted to run it? That's why I was calling. Grandma said she hadn't heard from you."

"Wait. Now I'm confused. I sent her a letter, a few weeks ago but I never heard back. I figured she was happy with the way things were and that she wasn't ready to give it over to someone else to manage."

"She called Sam. She asked him to let you know she was giving you the store. We've been clearing out the apartment upstairs. I got a fresh coat of paint up on all the walls." Paulie paused. "It's because Sam won't come home, right?"

"No! I didn't know. I am so sorry." The next words were the hardest to push past her tongue. "Sam never told me."

She choked down the sour taste in the back of her mouth. A rushing sound filled her ears and salty tears stung her eyes. She wanted to hug herself, to curl into the fetal position and rock until this horrid feeling of betrayal, that stabbed like a hundred knives, went away. A faint buzzing reminded Wynter she was still on the phone.

"Damn it! He knew a good thing when he saw it and he decided to keep you for himself," Paulie spat out.

A sob bubbled its way out, though she was quick enough to slap a hand over her mouth before Sam's sister could hear the keening wail that came right behind it.

"Aw, baby. My brother is an ass. Seriously. He's chickenshit for not facing the past. He needs to just get over himself and come back here, even just to drive through town without getting out of the car. Argh!"

Wynter winced as Paulie practically screamed her frustration.

Wiping her eyes and sniffing hard, she took a deep breath to try to calm the roiling snake pit that was her stomach.

"I want the job, Pauline. Is it still available?"

"The job. The apartment. Heck, Grandma Ruby is even throwing in her old Buick if you don't mind taking her to the occasional doctor's appointment."

"Can you come get me?" Her voice was eerily level, considering her current emotional state.

"Are you sure? I know I said he was an ass, but he's an ass that loves you, Wyn. You two have a good thing going and Grandma would understand if you'd rather stay with him."

"I was willing to give up my dream of running The Book Nook for him. I was willing to give up living in Scallop Shores. What was he willing to give up? Nothing. He deliberately kept me from achieving my goals, to suit his own selfish needs."

Charlotte's howl blared through the baby monitor on the desk and Wynter wanted to bawl along with her.

"I've got to go, Paulie. If you don't mind driving down to get us, I'd sure appreciate the lift."

"Call me when you're ready. And Wyn? I'm so sorry."

"You and me both, girlfriend."

Wynter ended the call, turned the volume down on the baby monitor and gave herself a few minutes to indulge in a crying jag that left her exhausted, her face swollen, and her head pounding.

But for the time being she was numb. And that was what would get her through what she had to do next.

...

His last precious few minutes left to spend with his girls and they weren't even here. Wynter had taken the baby over to Riley's to say goodbye. Searching frantically out the living room window, Sam waited for a glimpse of her before his sister arrived to pick them up. Not that it would matter. She'd said all she intended to say, and therefore wasn't speaking to him.

He tried to avoid looking at the pile of bags and boxes by the front door, a grim reminder that he had brought this all on himself. Already so close to losing it, Sam spied the little bunny he'd bought for Charlotte at the hospital, the day she'd been discharged after the doctor had determined her home birth a miraculous success. Snatching up the stuffed animal, he brought it to his cheek, struggling against the tears that choked off his airway.

This wasn't the way things were supposed to happen. They'd spent twelve years apart and they deserved their happily-ever-after. He was in, this time. He wasn't going to leave. He wasn't going to run. They were a family. Families stuck together.

Uh huh. So then why hadn't he had the decency to visit his grandmother in all these years? Why hadn't he spent time getting to know his nephews and the adult his sister had grown up to be? Why hadn't he gone to the resting place of his parents, to say goodbye, to tell them how sorry he was for not being there like he should have been? When it came to family, Sam sucked.

With a primal roar, ripped from the very center of his being, he threw the toy against the wall. As if to mock his pain, it barely made a sound, sliding to the floor in a fluffy heap. For one manic second, Sam looked around for something to break. Something that would make a more satisfying crash, cause damage worthy of the roiling emotions churning in his gut.

"Should we come back after you've finished your little tantrum?"

Crap.

Wynter hovered in the doorway, a protective arm slung across Charlotte's body. Her eyes were wary, red-rimmed from crying. She shifted from one foot to the other, frowning. She kept looking from the battered bunny to Sam and back again.

"I, um. You weren't supposed to see that."

"Clearly." She sniffed.

"Wyn, babe, I just wanted to say … "

"What, Sam? That you meant to tell me your grandmother offered me the job managing her store? You just never got around to it?"

She had him there. He ran both hands through his too-long hair, tugging hard when he got to the ends. He needed to hurt. He deserved to feel this pain. Grinding his teeth, he stared hard at the floor. What could he say at this point? Really?

"I love you. Does that count for anything?" He poured all his grief into his countenance and winced at the cold 'tsk' and shoulder shrug that he received.

"Love is wanting the best for someone. It means encouraging them to follow their dreams, not deliberately standing in the way of them."

"I was doing my best, Wyn. I know I've got major hang ups with regard to Scallop Shores. But I was trying to give you everything you wanted in the only way I knew how."

"You meant well, Sam. I get that." She snuggled the baby closer and gave him a watery smile. "But I can't settle again. Not this time."

She began to pace the room.

"I applied to UCLA just to be with you and Holt. I put my own dreams on hold to help Holt achieve his goals." She sank to the couch and leaned her head back against the cushions. "The Book Nook? That's all I've ever wanted. Not some store that I can make into my own."

"But The Book Nook is my grandmother's store. If you had another one, in another town, it would be completely yours. No preconceived ideas."

"Her ideas, what she had built that store up to be—that's what made it so special. Any other place would be … lacking. And if I were to try to set up shop in any other town, I'd be settling. I can't do that again, Sam.

I owe it to Charlotte to show her that a strong woman follows her dreams, that she doesn't sit back and let others decide her fate."

She sounded so reasonable, so calm, while she ripped his heart from his chest and stomped it into a bloody pulp on the floor. Sam stood motionless in the center of the room, knowing that any attempt to touch her would be rebuffed.

They turned as one at the crunch of tires on gravel, their gazes focusing on the SUV pulling into the driveway. Paulie was here. They were out of time. Sam's eyes narrowed when he realized his sister had rented a small U-Haul and was towing it behind her. There would be no second trips to pick up anything they couldn't fit.

He met his sister at the door, accepting her chastising glare with a slight nod before waving her into the living room on the right. She had to do the obligatory oohing and aahing over baby Charlotte. Fatherly pride had him puffing out his chest before he remembered he'd lost that right. He slumped against the doorframe and tried to view the scene in front of him as dispassionately as possible. It wasn't working.

"I should make a quick pit stop before the long ride." Wynter stood up. "Paulie, would you mind?" She started to hand the baby over.

"Wait! Can I hold her ... one last time? Please, Wyn?" He knew he was begging, knew he sounded pathetic. But he didn't care. He was desperate.

Without a word she placed Charlotte in his arms, ducking her head and stepping away quickly. She couldn't even stand to be near him anymore, it seemed. Sam blinked away the tears he was finding it harder and harder to hold at bay.

"What did you do, little brother?" Paulie whispered after Wynter had left the room.

"I blew a perfectly good thing. I had love, real love, for the first time in my life and I blew it."

"Oh, Sammie." Paulie rubbed his back and he had to jerk away, before he started bawling like the pathetic jerk he was.

"I'm going to start loading up the truck." She hurried from the room, thankfully realizing how close he was to losing it.

Sam sat down in his comfy old brown corduroy recliner. He laid Charlotte out on his legs and studied her miniscule features. Bright, alert brown eyes tracked his every move. Her midnight black hair came from Holt, but her pert little chin was all Wynter. Her perfect Cupid's bow mouth opened in a huge yawn that ended on a smile when she realized she had his undivided attention. This little thief had stolen his heart.

"So Riley says to tell you he hates your f'ing guts." Wynter stood in the doorway, clasping and unclasping her hands.

"He's going to have to get in line. I'm hating myself enough for all of us."

She came in, perched on the corner of the coffee table.

"I still love you, Sam. I understand why you did what you did. I'm not leaving because you didn't tell me about Ruby's offer."

"I know. I get it. You have to follow your dream. If you love something, set it free, right?" His bitter bark of laughter startled the baby on his lap.

They sat for a moment, neither knowing what to say to make the situation any less difficult.

Paulie came in for another load of baby gear before disappearing back out the door. Wynter bounced up and grabbed the Pack 'n Play in one hand and a large duffle bag of Charlotte's clothes and blankets in the other. Without a backward glance, she hefted them to the car. Since he couldn't pull Wynter into his arms like he so desperately needed, Sam drew her daughter against his chest and cuddled her for all he was worth.

Too soon the women had the SUV loaded down and were ready to hit the road. The weenie in him wanted to run in the house and hide, avoid saying goodbye. Paulie probably sensed this was the case, because she'd taken his hand and dragged him to the driver's side of the car.

"I love you, idiot brother. Don't make it so blasted hard to keep in touch with you." She wrapped her arms around him and squeezed, ending with a loud smacker of a kiss on his cheek.

"I love you, too, Paulie. Give the boys my love. Tell 'em Uncle Sam will have another demo ready for them by next month."

He shuffled around to the other side of the car. Wynter had settled the baby into the back, closed the door and was waiting for him before getting in.

"Come with us." Her voice held a tinge of desperation.

"I … "

"You can't. I know. Just had to try."

"Keep trying, Wyn. Don't give up on me." He pulled her into his arms, not the least bit embarrassed that his tears were soaking the top of her head.

"I love you, Sam. I wish we could find a way to make this work."

All he could do was nod, his throat only capable of making gurgling noises. He kissed her forehead and set her away from him. Her chin quivered as she appeared to try for a smile and didn't quite succeed. Quickly, she ducked into the SUV and strapped the seatbelt across her body. She wouldn't look at him.

Paulie backed out of the driveway, tooting once before driving away. Sam didn't want to go back inside, to his lonely house that had been swept clean of all traces of life, love, and everything good that had, however briefly, been his. He wouldn't be welcome at Riley's. Not yet.

On leaden legs, he scuffed up to the front door. Until a few months ago, this house had been his sanctuary, a place designed to keep the past at bay. Now it was his jail, where he would do his penance, punished for daring to give love a chance. He'd barely gotten the door closed behind him before he slid to the floor, giving in to the tears that would no longer be contained.

Chapter 19

It smelled the same as she remembered. The dusty old books with an almost sweet undertone. The new books, just out of their boxes, the ink still fresh. Wynter walked slowly through the bookstore that had been a part of Scallop Shores since its owner, Ruby, had been her own age. She stopped, here and there, to brush her fingertips against a cover, or thumb through an old favorite.

Ah, it felt good to be back. Paulie had helped her move into the apartment upstairs. Ruby was more than happy to watch Charlotte while the other women had unpacked both Wynter's meager belongings and her daughter's vast mountain of baby gear. Ruby had offered the furnished apartment as part of a salary package. Wynter had to remind herself that this was the opportunity of a lifetime.

Returning to the front of the store, Wynter leaned her elbows on the counter and stared moodily out the window. Everything was falling into place. All her dreams were coming true. This was what she'd wanted. Why did she feel so miserable, then? Ungrateful. That's what she was. An ungrateful leech.

The bell tinkled over the door and she pasted on a welcoming smile, standing up straight. Sam's grandmother, Ruby, backed into the store, pulling Charlotte's stroller with her.

"We're back," the older woman sang out. "This little gal is quite the social butterfly. She charmed everyone we met. Even that old fart, Tom Feeney, gushed over her."

"Old Man Feeney's still a grouch, huh? He needs the love of a good woman."

"No good woman would have him," Ruby scoffed.

"Seriously, though. What is that man's story? Was he jilted as a young guy? Someone kick his puppy?"

Ruby shut the door behind herself and wheeled the baby up to the counter. She shrugged out of her long cardigan and turned to hang it on the coat tree near the door. Slipping behind the register, she sank into the rocking chair nestled in the corner.

"Oh, don't get me started on that old coot. I think he came out of his mother's womb grousing over the living conditions."

"Still, I just wonder. Sam has this neighbor in Braeden. He was the biggest sourpuss when I first met him, really not pleasant at all. I think I grew on him." Wynter's smile was wistful.

"You miss him." Ruby rocked in her chair, the statement thrown out casually.

"Riley? He's a teddy bear now. Of course I miss him." She busied herself undoing the straps, tucking Charlotte against her shoulder and swaying.

"I meant Sam, sweetheart. You miss my grandson, don't you?" The old woman stopped the chair and aimed a steely look at her target.

Wynter turned away, swallowing hard against the sorrow that threatened to bubble up and over. She had no doubt Ruby would offer a friendly shoulder to cry on. She just wasn't ready for that. It was too soon. Her wounds too close to the surface. Taking a moment to compose herself, she breathed in through her nose, let it fill her diaphragm before pushing it through pursed lips. Finally, she was ready to return her attention to the conversation.

"I wish things had been different. Yes. I miss him." She'd been trying for composed, nonchalant. But her words had come out swollen, clogged with emotion. Every ounce of pain that she was feeling forced its way into the inflection. *Please don't offer me sympathy right now. I'll lose it. I really will.*

"Don't give up on him just yet, love. Not too long ago, Sam would have kicked you out of his house. Politely, mind you. But he wouldn't have allowed such a powerful reminder of his past to remain in his present."

"That's just it, Ruby. I didn't give him a choice." Wynter paced from one end of the counter to the other and back. "I called in the friend card, a promise he'd made to me when we were still kids."

"Make no mistake, dear. He would not have honored that promise years ago. Even given how much he loved you."

"Did everyone know about this, except me?" She wanted to snarl with frustration.

"Oh, Sam never told a soul how he felt. But I knew. His mother knew, too. We used to imagine what it would be like if the two of you got married. What your babies would look like." She smiled gently at Charlotte, snoozing on her mother's shoulder. "What he'd be like as a dad."

"He's an amazing dad."

It didn't even matter that Sam wasn't Charlotte's biological father. He'd helped her come into the world. He'd been there every day since, every day until she'd taken her little girl away from him. Oh, Sweet Mother Mary, what had she done?

"What am I going to do, Ruby?"

"Well, the front window display needs changing. I was thinking something with a Mother's Day theme, but it's your call. Have fun with it."

"No, I mean, what am I going to do about Sam? I feel like … " Hampered by the baby in her arms, she couldn't throw her hands up in the air like she longed to do.

"Like you shouldn't have left? Like you should have stayed in that podunk town in Vermont, no matter how bitter and miserable it made you?"

"It wasn't that bad." *No, that was a whopper if she'd ever told one.* Wynter couldn't even stop the giggle that reverberated on her tongue. "Okay, it was bad. Oh, Ruby, it's a horrible place to live. Think Old Man Feeney times … Well, whatever the population is. And the town, the architecture, it was lifeless. I expected everyone I ran into to be wearing drab, beige gunny sacks."

"I know." Ruby scowled. "Pauline and I drove out there shortly after Samuel bought the house. We didn't visit him, didn't want him to feel threatened in his new place, you understand? But we just wanted to know that he was okay.

"Braeden, Vermont." She shuddered. "Well, that's when we realized he wasn't okay. The depth of his guilt, his powerful need to punish himself. I guess I hadn't realized just how badly he suffered from survivor's guilt."

"I guess it's pointless to ask if he ever sought help for it?" Wynter set the baby down on the polished honey countertop and tickled her tummy.

"Why get help for something you think you deserve?" Both women sighed and nodded.

"So, whatcha got planned for that window display? You've been itching to design one of those since you were ten years old."

Wynter stared out the window at the town of Scallop Shores. This had been her dream for so long. Only now her dream had morphed to include Sam. Her little family, her life, would not be complete without Sam. But Sam was in Vermont and had no intention of ever stepping foot in the town that held his most sorrowful memories. She had left him to prove to herself that she would not settle for anything less than her heart's desire. But wasn't that exactly what she'd ended up doing?

• • •

"I'm selling the house," Sam announced upon letting himself into Riley's house—after the man had purposely slammed the door in his face.

"Running from your memories again?" Riley spun his chair around and glared at his best friend. "Where's it going to be this time? Alaska? Siberia? How long are you going to keep running, Sam?"

"I'm not running *from*, buddy of mine. I'm running *to*."

He ducked into the kitchen to help himself to a cup of coffee, decided his nerves were already shot, and opted for a glass of water from the tap. Riley appeared in the wide doorframe, a skeptical frown knotting his eyebrows together. Sam coated his parched throat before continuing.

"I need to get her back, man."

"There is only one way to get her back and you swore you'd never go there."

"That was before I thought I had a chance with her. Before I remembered how important family is." He set the empty glass on the counter with a thunk, threading a shaky hand through his hair. "God, Ri, I could have hidden out here until Paulie called to tell me my grandmother had died. Seriously, what kind of grandson am I?"

"A crappy one," Riley admitted.

"No doubt. And a crappy brother and a crappy uncle. A crappy overall person." He resisted the urge to pound a fist into the nearest cabinet. It wasn't his house, after all.

"Uh huh. And what makes you think Wynter is going to want this crappy person in her happy, shiny new life?"

"She's not. I get that. She doesn't want the Sam-with-baggage. But if I can prove to her that I'm ready to change."

"Dude, I want to believe you. I do. But I heard her ask you, so many times, to join her in Scallop Shores. You wouldn't even discuss it. You shut her down. And now that she's called your bluff, you're all ready to go racing after her and pick up where you left off. I don't buy it."

Riley clucked his tongue and frowned into his lap before looking up and spearing Sam with a sharp glance.

"What are you going to do? Buy a house in the next town over and try to coax Wynter to live with you there and still get to work in her dream town?" He sounded like he was trying to draw out a confession.

"Fine, don't believe me. But I'm moving back to Scallop Shores and you're coming with me."

"The hell I am!"

Riley backed his chair up and sped down the hall to the living room, not stopping until he reached the furthest shelf of books. His back to his friend, he chose a book at random, plucked it off the shelf and pretended to get lost in a battle scene. Sam rolled his eyes.

"You have no ties to this place. We'll find another place. Somewhere we can be together."

"Dude, you want me or Wynter? 'Cause it sounds like you're not sure which side of the closet you're on. I think you're trying to make me feel better about you taking off, but I gotta tell ya—just feelin' a little squicky here."

"Oh, shut up, already. I am moving to Scallop Shores. And like it or not, you are part of our family. You're coming with us. End of story."

"I'm a lone wolf. I don't play well with others." Riley slammed the book shut, heaved a sigh and turned around.

They eyed each other, neither one offering to back down.

"Besides, I just got this sweet new set up for my books. I'm not going anywhere without my built-ins. You can't get my built-ins into a new house, I'm not budging."

"You're the biggest pain in my ass. You know that?" Sam slapped a hand against his denim-clad thigh.

"Wynter went to a lot of trouble to build these for me. They are custom made for a custom guy." Riley ran a hand along one of the wheels of his chair.

"I bet if you ask nicely, she'd do it again. She seems to get a kick out of using power tools." And he got an endless thrill out of watching her use them.

"You don't need me around, mucking up your alone time. I'll be fine here. I've got my nurse and my PT to check up on me, make sure I'm not dead."

"God, you're such a whiner!" Sam cuffed his friend upside his head and was rewarded with a nasty epithet.

"Truth be told, Wynter probably wouldn't take me back if I didn't have you in tow."

At this, Riley snorted. "Heh heh. I can see that. I'm your ace in the hole. Oh, the power." The resulting laughter sounded more like a deranged cackle. This time Sam smacked a palm against his own head. Pain in the ass, indeed!

•••

His hands were fused to the steering wheel with perspiration, almost like a built in fail-safe to keep him in his SUV, driving toward his goal. He'd begun to mutter to himself somewhere between the NH tolls and the Welcome to Maine—The Way Life Should Be sign. He longed for a paper bag—whether to soothe his rapid breathing or to puke in, he wasn't yet sure.

Riley's voice was in his head, jeering and obnoxious. *"You swore you'd never go back. You can't do it. Not even for Wynter."* Sam's muttering turned to swearing, railing at the friend who had stayed behind to deal with the sale of not one, but two houses. He could use a friend here with him now.

No! He'd brought this on himself, staying away so long it made it that much more difficult to come home again. He was right to come alone. No one knew he was coming. It was better this way. In case he chickened out. Sam sneered at the negative thought. He wasn't going to chicken out. He was finally ready.

All too soon, the exit for Scallop Shores loomed in front of him. The urge to drive on by was strong and Sam had to give an extra tug on the steering wheel to nudge the car toward the off ramp. He was here. He was doing this. He felt like he was going to die.

It would be hell for a while. He hadn't expected it to be easy, just because Wynter and Charlotte were here. He'd done some research before leaving and found a therapist in Scallop Shores who could help him process the mountain of emotional garbage that he'd managed to barricade himself behind for the last twelve years. He'd meant it when he told Riley that he didn't expect Wynter to take back the old Sam. She deserved a new Sam. A Sam with his head on straight and no guilt or drama weighing him down.

The old Chamber of Commerce, a sad shack, really, had been torn down. It had been replaced by a much larger, more sophisticated building. Sam liked the row of Adirondacks on the porch. Welcome to Scallop Shores, they seemed to say. Sit a spell. He felt his blood pressure start to slow. Just a bit.

Turning left at the last stoplight before hitting the heart of the town, Sam drove down Main Street. Finding it remarkably unchanged, he wasn't sure if he ought to feel relieved or anxious that it would stir up unwanted memories. The First Congregational Church, with its gorgeous white spire, was still the tallest building downtown. The Civil War statue still stood at attention, forcing cars to slow down and enjoy the scenery as they navigated that turn.

Coming up on the right was the historic residence that had housed his dad's vet clinic. Sam's eyes were drawn to the old yellow building. Heart thudding in his chest, he read the words on the sign hanging above the door: DENNIS VETERINARY CLINIC. Someone had taken it over, yet they'd still kept the name. Hot tears pricked at his eyelids even as he couldn't stop the grin from sliding into place. His dad would have liked that.

Shops lined both sides of the streets. Some he remembered from his youth, others were new to him. Logan's Bakery was still there.

Thank God. He hoped they still made their killer bear claw pastries. Tiny Treasures. That was new. Sam scrunched his eyes, the better to peer inside the storefront window from the SUV. Baby stuff. Should he run in and get a gift for Charlotte before he arrived at the bookstore? Should he stop and pick up flowers for Wynter?

Yeah, he should do all of that. But, quite frankly, he didn't want to put off seeing them a moment longer. His girls wouldn't expect gifts. They'd just be happy that he was there. His girls. His family. Sam focused his attention on finding a parking spot. It was family reunion time.

He wiped his palms on the seat of his jeans, cracked the kinks out of his neck and willed his stomach to stop flopping around in his gut like a beached fish. He'd managed to park a few shops down and hadn't run into anyone he knew on the short walk up the street.

Now he stood in front of The Book Nook. He started to turn the handle on the door but caught a glimpse of the window display and was drawn toward it. It was a cozy nursery scene, complete with rug and a rocking chair. Seated in the rocking chair was a male mannequin, the father, presumably. Only Sam felt like he was looking in a mirror.

The father held an infant in one arm and a tattered paperback in the other. *The Hobbit*. It was him and Charlotte. Wynter had chosen something very personal for her first window display. Choked up, Sam reached out to touch the glass. Did she realize the depth of the love that was conveyed in this simple grouping of items?

"If you love something, set it free." Wynter had snuck up beside him. She slipped her hand into his.

"I thought that something was you. And I didn't see you coming back to me."

"Nope. That something was you. And you did come back. It is meant to be."

"Everything I could ever want is in Scallop Shores. Or will be soon." Sam gave her hand a squeeze.

"Okay, now you lost me." She tugged him inside the store.

"Riley. The grumpiest member of our strange little family."

Wynter squealed then slapped his arm. "Our little family is not strange! It's perfect." She furrowed her brow. "How are we going to get Riley upstairs?"

"We aren't. I bought a duplex out on Bartlett Road. They've agreed to make the whole thing ADA accessible. Riley would be able to come and go whenever he likes."

"But, Sam, it's so close to … " She stuffed a knuckle in her mouth to keep from saying the rest.

"My parents' old place? I know. And thanks for the concern. But if I'm going to live in Scallop Shores, I can't exactly avoid that area for the rest of my life. I can do this, Wyn."

"I'm so ashamed." She cast her eyes to the floor. "I doubted you'd come back."

"Don't worry about it. I probably doubted myself a heck of a lot more."

"I guess if you are facing your demons then I'll have to face mine."

"You mean the demons that live in Florida?" Sam chuckled. "Seeing them a time or two a year won't be so bad. Charlotte should have the chance to get to know *all* her relatives."

"Yeah, well I knew you'd find your way home. Now come over here and give your grandmother a long twelve years' worth of hugs and kisses." Ruby stood in front of the counter, hands on her hips.

"Just a minute, Grandma. There is something I have to do first."

And he gathered Wynter into his arms, spinning them around until they were both breathless. Lifting her off her feet, he touched his lips to hers, pouring all his love, all his intentions, all his incredible joy into the kiss. He was home to stay.

About the Author

Jennifer DeCuir lives in the Pacific Northwest with her husband, two children, and three neurotic pets. She dreams of sunny days and wishes Starbucks would deliver to her front door.

More from This Author
(From *Five of Hearts* by Jennifer DeCuir)

"Running away" was such a cowardly term. Dean preferred to think of it as "permanently relocating." Lying back, he breathed in a gulp of fresh Maine air, laced with pine and beach roses and the sharp tang of the Atlantic Ocean. He felt his muscles relax, really relax, as he sank deeper into the hammock. He'd waited almost half his life for this.

At fourteen years old, Dean had willingly forfeited his anonymity—and the peace and quiet that went with it—for the chance to become an internationally revered pop star. He'd become Dino Valentine, lead singer of the boy band Five of Hearts. For the next six years, Dean's life had been a whirlwind of recording sessions, hours of choreography, concert dates, and appearances.

Fame. Fortune. The perks that came with being a household name. It all sounded great in the beginning, but no one ever told him about the downside of being under the microscope. All the people who wanted their share of the pie, their moment in the spotlight, their chance to spend someone else's hard earned money. And the devious ways they plotted to get it.

In the six years since the band had broken up, Dean had kept to himself as much as possible, and tried to stay out of the public eye. He didn't leave his Malibu mansion except to go visit his band mates. He was content to spend his days writing music, swimming laps in the pool, and chasing off opportunistic photogs looking for the chance to catch Dean in a compromising position—the money shot that would set them up for life.

Now, in the midst of yet another groundless paternity suit, Dean knew he needed to go where the money-grubbing vultures couldn't find him. He was done with the life of a celebrity. He was done with Southern California.

He swung from the hammock in his new backyard, a plate of cookies and an ice cold beer within reach. His baseball cap was pulled low over his eyes to block out the glare of the sun. A group of tall arborvitae bushes hid the next house from view, giving Dean the illusion that he was truly alone, something he'd been craving for so long. He opened the book in his lap but stared at the words, unseeing. He hoped all these changes, the cross-country move, and buying a new house, would bring him the sense of peace that had been missing.

Several years ago, Dean had had a tutor who came from Maine. He'd listen for hours while the man talked about what a beautiful state it was. He'd hailed from the coast and spent summers helping on his dad's lobster boat. He had told Dean all about the snowmobiling, the ice fishing, bonfires, and parties in the woods. He'd described the crisp tang of autumn in the air and the riot of color from the trees, almost the entire month of October. There was something to do all year round.

Dean closed his eyes and breathed deeply of the fresh mown grass, ocean breezes, and a flowering shrub he couldn't put a name to. He dug a toe into the lawn and set his hammock gently swinging. Smacking his lips, he grinned in drowsy happiness. He was falling asleep in the middle of the day. What a foreign concept that had become. Dean pillowed his head on his arm and snuggled into the hammock for some rest. Just as he was drifting off he thought he heard giggling.

Cracking one eye open, Dean scanned the yard. There, over by the blueberry bushes, was a carrot-topped little pixie. He shook his head, opening his other eye, and looked again. This time the tiny child was over by the willow tree, crouched down and grinning. Dean rubbed his eyes and leaned out of the hammock for a better look. Wait. Now the little thief was right beside him—stealing his cookies! How could he be everywhere at once?

Dean reached out to grab him by the collar but forgot he was in the hammock and lost his balance. The miniature con artist screeched as Dean nearly fell on top of him. He took off, a cookie in each hand. Dean landed with a thud on the lawn.

"Hey, get back here with my cookies!" Dean tried to get up to run after the child but tripped over his own feet and landed face first in the turf, knocking his ball cap off his head.

"Problems?" A soft, feminine voice, thickly laced with humor, called from the edge of the lawn.

Dean stood, brushing his clothes off. He was starting to think chasing off paparazzi was preferable to chasing after … was it only a child? So much for peace and quiet.

"That kid made off with my cookies." He scanned the perimeter of the yard, unable to locate the cookie thief.

"That team works fast. I imagine your cookies have been gobbled up by now." He could actually hear the amused smile in her voice.

That team? There was more than one? Dean was starting to get a headache.

"How'd you all get into my yard anyway?" Rubbing his temples, he tried to work out how he'd thought there was one kid darting through his shrubs only to find there were more. How many more? This was confusing.

"There is a break in the hedge. I have a finely tuned radar when it comes to this bunch. I had a feeling they were up to no good."

Frowning, Dean snatched up the empty plate. He turned, finally prepared to square off with this latest intruder. His words stuck to his tongue. His gaze was drawn to a pair of startlingly blue eyes. A light breeze picked up a strand of her long red hair, tossing it around playfully. Red hair and freckles. Suddenly, he was back in grade school remembering his first crush. Oh, he was a goner.

She smiled, shrugging her shoulders in apology. The twinkle in her eyes called the sincerity of the apology into question, yet somehow Dean didn't mind.

"My name is Shannon. I live next door with those … cookie thieves."

"I, um, I'm Dean." His brain was working overtime, trying to catch up. "Just how many kids are running around here?"

"Brady, Brenna, and Brian, you march those little butts out here right this second!"

Dean watched in horror as not one, but three little children peered out from behind the tall hedge and proceeded to line up in front of Shannon for inspection. He didn't know much about kids, but he'd guess them to be about four or five years old. Their heads were bowed but Dean could tell they weren't the least bit repentant. There were cookie crumbs on their cheeks and they looked to be trying very hard not to giggle.

Grudgingly, he had to admit they were cute—for thieving little cookie heathens. The little girl, Brenna, looked him right in the eye and winked. Dean focused on his sneakers, trying not to let the munchkin charm him.

"What do you have to say for yourselves?" Shannon eyed them all, her face stern, and her features grim.

"We're sorry, mister," they offered in unison. Dean doubted that was the first time they'd had to apologize for something like this.

"It's okay, I guess. You owe me some new cookies, though." He folded his arms across his chest and cast a forlorn glance at the empty plate. He really had been looking forward to those cookies.

"That's right, kiddos. You are going to spend tomorrow afternoon in the kitchen with me. No outdoors time until we get a nice batch of … " She offered him an opening.

"Chocolate chip—no nuts."

"Right. You all will be baking chocolate chip cookies, with no nuts, for Mr. Dean. You will not cut through the gap in the bushes to deliver them, but will instead use the walkway, like civilized neighbors."

Shannon silenced the groans of disappointment with a single look. Dean was impressed. She sent the children on their way back to their own yard and turned to him. He stood still while she gave him the once over, his nerves on edge as he waited to see if she'd recognize him. He panicked, reaching up to his bare head, when he realized he wasn't wearing his hat. He always wore a hat.

Shannon looked like she was in her mid-twenties, just the right age to have been a fan when Five of Hearts was at the top of their fame. If she recognized him, it would blow any chance of his hiding out in blessed anonymity in this quaint seaside town. Instead, she merely ducked her head shyly and played with the hem of her shirt. Whew. Maybe he was in the clear.

"Sorry about that heathen crack. They're cute kids. Are they triplets? You must be the older sister, then."

"Thank you ... to the cute kids *and* to the older sister bit. That wasn't necessary. Totally welcome, mind you, but not necessary. Nope, they're all mine." She blushed.

"Wow. I can't even imagine one kid, but three at once? What did your husband say when you guys found out you were having triplets?"

"In a word? Goodbye." Shannon shrugged, feigning indifference. "Let's just say he didn't find himself up to the challenge."

"What a slimeball!" Dean clapped a hand over his mouth, embarrassed that he'd let that judgment be voiced aloud.

What kind of man would abandon his children? It was something Dean had been accused of many times—but something he would never do, if a child were actually his.

Dean hadn't been quite seventeen years old when he was named in his first paternity suit. He hadn't been an angel, but he'd been careful. His manager had drilled it into all of them just how important it was to use protection. Dean had known the girl was lying. And yet he'd been advised to settle out of court, pay the girl what she wanted, and keep it out of the news.

But when this latest paternity suit surfaced, he knew he couldn't keep paying off these women and hoping the problem would just go away. He needed to take a stand, and stop the madness once and for all.

Shannon's trill of laughter was music to his ears.

"Eh, I like to look at it as him doing us a favor." Shannon turned toward the opening in the hedge. "Listen, I'm really sorry the kids invaded your space like this. It's just that they were used to playing over here. The house has been on the market for years. This just kind of became an extension of our backyard. I'll try to keep them out of here in the future."

"Yeah, okay." Dean watched her duck her head and pass through the tight space in the bushes.

This new life was not shaping up to be the tranquil escape he'd been looking for. He'd sworn off women—especially women that showed up on his doorstep with a child. Triplets! Screw the Arborvitae. He was going to have to build a fence. A really tall one.

Dean went back to his hammock and tried again to take that nap. If he heard sweet harp music in the background, he paid it no heed. He dreamed of tiny pixies with crumbs on their cheeks surrounding a beautiful fairy queen with gossamer wings and long, bright red hair.

• • •

The three little cookie thieves had been fed, bathed, and sent to bed early for stealing from their new neighbor. Shannon should have welcomed the extra quiet time but she found herself restless, unable to relax. Normally able to calm her racing brain with nimble fingers, she was frustrated when crocheting didn't seem to work. She set the afghan-in-progress aside.

Heading to her cozy little kitchen, Shannon stood on tiptoe and tried to catch a glimpse of the big house next door. She could just make out a twinkle or two of lights through the thick hedging as her new neighbor settled in for the evening. Dean. His name was Dean.

Dust flew as she drew her curtains closed for the first time, not for privacy but to shut out the obsessive thoughts that had been plaguing her since she'd met the annoyingly hot Malibu Ken lookalike that afternoon. Seriously, the guy must have come from Southern California, with that deep tan. Did he surf all day? How did he afford one of the luxury summer homes in Scallop Shores? Screenwriter? Actor? He didn't look like anyone she'd ever seen in the movies. But then again, when was the last time she'd been to the movies? It must have been at least five years.

It was a cool evening in her tiny little caretaker's cottage, behind the huge summer house of her employer, Ms. Sheffield. Shannon perched on the edge of a wooden chair at the table. She wrapped her fingers around the mug of tea she'd fixed and stared down into the whirling steam. It was May and things were starting to get busier in the little tourist town of Scallop Shores, Maine. Ms. Sheffield would probably make an appearance over the holiday weekend. Shannon needed to get the big house ready for her arrival.

She'd be eternally grateful to the wealthy Wall Street mogul who had taken a chance on a very pregnant, single mom, who had never even been to college. Ms. Sheffield had never married, never had children, so Shannon had been flummoxed when the old woman took them under her wing. Last spring, after the muddy season was over, she'd had a huge play area built in the backyard, with swings and a slide, a sandbox, and a climbing wall. Shannon had offered to have it taken out of her paycheck, a little each week, but Ms. Sheffield wouldn't hear of it.

But the successful businesswoman was in her seventies now, and the weekends she hosted at her summer home were getting fewer and farther between. What would happen if she sold the place? Or worse, what if she died? She didn't have family to leave it to. Where did that leave Shannon and her kids? She'd gotten too comfortable with their easy life. She didn't have a back-up plan.

Agitated, Shannon carried her tea to the sink and dumped it out. She quickly rinsed the mug and set it in the drying rack. Tapping her fingers on the edge of the counter she looked around for some busy work. The counters were clean. The stove, oven, and refrigerator were spotless. She headed for the living room, certain to have something to do there. The Legos were all neatly put away. Brenna's tea set was on its tray, all the pieces together. Not even a stray sock lying on the floor. She blew out a long sigh and pursed her lips.

She wasn't usually on edge like this. Rolling her shoulders to try to work out some of the tension, Shannon trod quietly down the hall. She peeked her head around the half-open door to Brenna's room. One leg hung off the bed and her monkey was clutched tightly to her side. Shannon slipped in and slid the skinny leg back beneath the covers.

Across the hall, the boys slept in twin beds, side by side, a Batman nightlight in between. Brian snored softly while Brady muttered in his sleep. Shannon felt that familiar clutch in her heart, that same one she'd experienced for the first time as she held each of her new babies. It had never been her intention to raise such a large family alone. But life didn't always work out the way you would expect. Shannon learned the hard way that she didn't need a man.

The fact that a man just happened to have moved into the house that had been vacant as long as she'd lived here should not have rattled her the way it did. So what if he was good looking? Big deal that he could be about her age. They were polar opposites and she'd do well to remember that. Mr. Perfect Dean was some sort of trust fund baby and she was a glorified maid. She didn't need a man. She didn't need a neighbor who happened to be a man. Disgusted that she was putting way too much thought into this, Shannon headed back down the hall—to scrub her perfectly clean kitchen.

Also check out *Drawn to Jonah* by Jennifer DeCuir.

In the mood for more Crimson Romance?
Check out *California Thyme* by Casey Dawes at
CrimsonRomance.com.